Praise for *The Oblivion Room*

The Oblivion Room is, simply put, one of the best collections of short stories I've ever read. Remember that feeling you got the first time you read Ray Bradbury, or Stephen King, or Shirley Jackson, how magical the prose felt? Well, get ready to experience that magic again, because Christopher Conlon has it in spades. The stories presented here are absolutely fantastic. I devoured them all, and I'm willing to bet you will too. Along with Laird Barron and John Langan, Christopher Conlon is carrying the torch for literary horror in the 21st century. Pay attention, because Conlon is one of our best, hands down."

—Bram Stoker Award Winner **Joe McKinney**,
author of *Mutated* and *Inheritance*

"Reading Christopher Conlon's stories made me think of the first time I tasted Laphroaig single malt scotch. 'People actually drink this—voluntarily? *For pleasure?!*' It's hard to take, the flavor is so intense. But for those with the strength to handle it, there's nothing better...The short stories in *The Oblivion Room* carry hints and suggestions of Poe, of Kafka, of the Japanese writer Tarō Harei, and occasionally of Richard Matheson. But it is in the novella 'Welcome Jean Krupa, World's Greatest Girl Drummer!' that Conlon's talent shines most brightly. In this long tale he explores the world of music (and he gets it right) and the nature of human love and commitment and tragedy (and he gets this very right). A fine, memorable book."

—Hugo and Left Coast Crime Lifetime Achievement Award Winner
Richard A. Lupoff, author of
ler and *Dreams*

"Christopher Conlon's latest collection, *The Oblivion Room*, represents dark fiction at its finest. These are richly imagined tales of loss, told with impeccable, devastating tone. There is joy here as well, in the exhilarating buildup to the collection's superb novella, 'Welcome Jean Krupa, World's Greatest Girl Drummer!' or in the characters' isolated, deluded moments of escape—before their personal Oblivion Rooms draw them back in. With this literate and poignant collection, Conlon proves once again that he's a true poet of melancholy."

—Bram Stoker Award Winner **Norman Prentiss**, author of *Invisible Fences* and *The Fleshless Man*

"Since the publication of his acclaimed first novel, *Midnight on Mourn Street* (2008), Conlon has quickly established himself as one of the preeminent names in contemporary literary horror. His newest collection of short fiction showcases his penchant for bending genre conventions in imaginative and provocative new ways. In the title story, a woman with little memory of her former life finds herself imprisoned in a pitchblack cell and struggles to keep her sanity by writing a journal entirely in her head. 'Skating the Shattered Glass Sea' tells the story of a dying businessman who pays a visit to the asylum where his mentally ill twin sister, unseen for more than 50 years, is still erecting the imaginary castles they created together as children. The protagonist in 'Grace' revisits the childhood home and small closet where an abusive stepfather kept her confined with her fantasies. Every piece in the volume bears the stamp of Conlon's gift for combining subtle terror with unforeseeable plot twists. Connoisseurs of cutting-edge horror will not want to miss it."

—**Carl Hays**, *Booklist*

THE OBLIVION ROOM

Stories of Violation

Christopher Conlon

Evil Jester Press

New York

ALSO BY CHRISTOPHER CONLON

NOVELS
Lullaby for the Rain Girl
A Matrix of Angels
Midnight on Mourn Street

SHORT FICTION
Herding Ravens
Thundershowers at Dusk: Gothic Stories
Saying Secrets

POETRY
Starkweather Dreams
Mary Falls: Requiem for Mrs. Surratt
The Weeping Time
Gilbert and Garbo in Love

THEATER
Midnight on Mourn Street: A Play in Two Acts

AS EDITOR
A Sea of Alone: Poems for Alfred Hitchcock
He Is Legend: An Anthology Celebrating Richard Matheson
Poe's Lighthouse
The Twilight Zone Scripts of Jerry Sohl
Filet of Sohl

TABLE OF CONTENTS

The Oblivion Room

◯◯◯

1. A Beginning

I will remember this. I'll remember it all. I must. Over and over, again and again I'll repeat the words until they're tattooed into my blood, my bones, my DNA—words, sentences, paragraphs spinning invisibly around in my head and yet locked down tight in a special room of memory reserved just for the purpose. I will remember this. I'll remember it all. I must.

The Greek bards memorized heroic epics that, written out, take up hundreds of pages—*The Iliad* and *The Odyssey* both complete in one individual's mind, with any particular section available at an instant's recall for an audience that wanted to hear it sung. Of course the likes of Homer had the advantages of poetry, rhyme and steady meter, to help them. But what I must remember won't take hundreds of pages. It can't. Before it can run anything like that length I'll be dead. Or gone from this place. One way or another, my words will stop.

I will remember this. I'll remember it all. I must. I have no computer, no typewriter, no paper, no pencil, no pen. I suppose I could gnaw open a fingertip and scrawl on the stone in my blood, but even then I have no light. Smeared blood on black walls: the same as nothing, the same as silence. All I have is this, then. My journal. My journal of the brain.

◙◙◙

It's taken me hours to memorize all those words, but I have them now and I can move on.

Hours? Perhaps it was hours, but I have no way of knowing. It could have been minutes or days. Yet I think it was hours, maybe two or three. It's a guess, that's all, based on how long I think it would have taken me to memorize that number of words back then, in the other world. I start again and then again, *I will remember this. I'll remember it all. I must.* And then forward. Sometimes aloud, often silently. Silently is the greater challenge, and I dislike hearing my own voice here, in this dark. It's grown husky and hollow and when I first found myself in this place I spent so much time screaming that my throat was burned raw and my voice ripped to a whisper. To hear it now only reminds me of those first days and fills me with despair, the very thing I'm trying to avoid with this journal. It's vital to keep my mind active, engaged. Before I decided to start this word-project I was aware of slippage, of sometimes becoming unhinged, seeing things I couldn't possibly see, things that could not be there. Hearing things, too. At first it was desperately tempting to believe in it all, that the things were real, yet a deeper part of me knew that I was beginning to hallucinate, my mind in its frantic bewilderment creating for itself what wasn't there. It was then, in those times when I came back to reality from whatever deranged vision I'd had, that I knew I had to do something, keep my mind from flying off in a million schizoid directions. Otherwise at some point I would no longer be able to come back at all.

I knew a journal would help me. I kept one as a girl, pouring whatever shoddy secrets I had onto its virginal white pages. Its cover, I remember, was festooned with flowers, irises and orchids. The journal had been a present from an otherwise indifferent aunt, one with whom I had no relationship of any note then or ever. And yet it proved to be a sublime gift, the greatest of my life, for it gave me the habit of journal-writing, the mental discipline to transform experience into words. At times as an aid to memory I sit cross-legged on the floor and lean forward, as if a physical journal lay before me, and "write" in it with my thumb and index finger forming an invisible pen. It helps—the physical act of writing, even if no words actually materialize on the floor. Then again, in this dark, how would I know?

2. Where I Live

It would be tempting to say, "I can't tell you, because I don't know." And that is literally true. Yet I've learned a great deal about this place in the time I've been here. At first it was only darkness, utter darkness, with hard walls everywhere around me. I can see quite literally nothing. There are times even now, with all the mental discipline I've been able to bring, that this still causes me to panic. The sensation is not unlike being buried alive, I imagine. My heart punches my chest, my breath comes short, and if I'm unable to bring myself under control I find myself screaming hysterically again, hurling my body against the wall, pounding the floor, tearing at my hair, finally curling up in a tight exhausted ball, eyes clenched shut, arms sheltering my head. Again and again I've done this. The curling-up seems to be the only thing that can keep me in such times from feeling like some enormous weight is pressing me down, leaving me trapped and breathless. In earlier days I would have smashed my head against the wall and floor so hard that as I cradled it later in its ringing pain I would taste blood running across my cheeks into my mouth and perhaps fall unconscious for a time. Now I rarely lose control to this level, some part of me now limiting the damage I do to myself.

This journal helps. I have no idea how long it has taken me to memorize all I've put down so far. Days? Weeks? Yet it fills the time magnificently, keeps me focused and away from the panic that always seems to lurk under my consciousness, ready to spring.

So: where I live. I live in a cylindrical room which seems to be, as near as I can measure, about fifteen feet across. There are no corners anywhere, nothing to break the slick, curved, gently bumpy sensation under my hands of what I've decided must be glossily-painted brick. The floor is cement, completely smooth but lacking the gloss of the walls and so most likely unpainted. I have no idea how high the ceiling is, but it must be very high. When I shout I can hear reverberations ascending what sounds like forever. I've tried tossing things—bits of food—high into the air to determine if I can strike the ceiling with them, but to no avail.

The only thing that breaks the perfect monotony of the wall and floor is something I've come to notice only recently. There is a crack in the floor. It's quite narrow, and only perhaps five or six inches long, running in a rough zigzag from the place where the wall joins the floor out toward the center of the cylinder. The crack is so small and shallow that it can be hard to find it when I want to—it's hardly there at all. But it's there. I can spend hours running over it with my fingers, seeing if I can break away any little bits that might make it that much wider. (Thus far I've failed.) It's one of the main things I do while going over the words in this journal again and again and again in my mind.

3. How I Live

One illusion I allow myself is to pretend that I'm blind. Just all at once, I insist within my mind, I woke up and my sight was completely gone, nothing but blackness before me. Like anyone in that position, I went through moments of panic, but I learned to adjust, to start living not by my eyes but my ears, my nose, my tongue, my skin. Sometimes I believe it, at least for a while.

I have no clothes. I run my hands over myself at times, pretend that the sensation is that of a coat or a skirt or a pair of socks being pulled over me. I try to remember the tactile sensation of, say, a cotton shirt on my skin, or a corduroy jacket. I try to remember what it felt like to walk in heels, high heels, low ones, or in slippers or sandals. What silk panties felt like slipping up over my bottom, the elastic snapping my waist. A hat on my head, a scarf on my neck. Anything. Sometimes I feel I would give anything I ever had for just that, even a scarf, anything at all that I could put on any part of my body just to cover *something*, to be able to say, "This is mine. You can't see it. You can't have it. It is not yours." But I have nothing. Most of the time I don't think of it because of my total blind-dark anyway. But it's cold here. I don't believe the temperature is absolutely steady, however—there are times when I feel only a bit chilled, and there are others when I fear I'll die from it, holding myself, shivering uncontrollably, engulfed in goose flesh, sometimes lying down on the floor and curling up but then after a few minutes jumping up again, hopping from foot to foot because the floor is intolerably frigid. I think it's like this for days sometimes. I run, dance, do jumping jacks, shadow-box until I'm exhausted. I know I'll pay for this, too: sweat forms on my skin and then slowly grows icy. Yet I cannot exercise forever and so finally I drop down and try to put my mind somewhere else, somewhere far away. I "write" in this journal. I run whole movies in my mind, adding scenes or changing events as I wish. I listen to entire albums. It's better than what I used to do in such situations, which would be to run head-first into the wall as many times as it took to pass out. I have a perpetual headache now, of course, and my neck suffers shooting pains which feel like sudden tiny jolting electrocutions. There is a ringing in my ears that comes and goes. I did all this to myself.

Of course there is the question of food, one which I still find baffling. Despite all my efforts, I have been unable to discover where it comes from, or when, or from whom. Yet it appears. I'm convinced that there must be a panel in the wall that rises to allow in the tray, but I've never found any evidence of such a thing. I've tried to stay awake as long as I can, remaining stock-still the whole time, knowing that when the food is delivered there must be *some* sound, however brief, however quiet, and once I almost thought I heard something, a slight *shush* and *thump*, but I'd been waiting so long that I might have dreamed these sounds. There was food then, on the other side of the cylinder; but it might have been there for hours if I'd been sleeping, and the sounds were a fantasy.

On the tray, which seems to be an ordinary plastic tray, will generally be three separate things. One is a small container, also plastic, a kind of carafe filled with lukewarm water. The second is a small plate, plastic again, with a few items of food on it, usually some vague sort of gruel, cold and viscous. I detect its beginnings as oatmeal, but other things have been tossed into it, like someone's random leftovers:

fruit peels, carrot shavings, bread crusts, grisly little bits of what might once have been meat. Sometimes there are tough chunks which I'm not sure are, properly speaking, *food* at all. If I can chew them, I eat them. No utensils of any kind are provided, ever; I simply push my lips to the lips to the pile and swallow what's there, finally licking the plate clean.

The third item on the tray is a plastic pot whose foul odor leaves no doubt as to its purpose. There is no cover, so the smell permeates the cylinder; the food plate is too small to cover the opening. The pot is only there when the food arrives, and is taken away—when? how? I have never been able to determine. But, along with the other things, it is taken away each evening (I think of the meals I receive as coming once every twenty-four hours, though I have no evidence for this, and I've chosen to think of the meal as "dinner," hence "evening"). If I try to hold onto it, as I did once, no further food or water arrive. The fact that it's taken away of course means I'm left without a toilet, and some of the most agonizing hours I have spent here have been spent desperately holding onto myself, trying to push back what so needs to escape me, trying to keep from letting my piss or shit burst out onto the floor. I think this is the worst of it, worse than the cold or hunger or darkness. The humiliation of having to squat on my own floor (insofar as anything here is "my own") and then, in utter blackness, carefully avoid the spot for however long it takes for dinner to come around again, at which time I can carefully lift any fecal matter into the pot with my fingers, thus being forced to waste some of the vital carafe of water to at least rinse my fingertips. Whatever urine I've left simply must dry there, though at times I have used a bit of the water in the carafe to attempt to clean the spot a little. (The smell I simply live with; the truth is, I hardly notice it anymore.) At least I've never had my period since being here, so that is not a problem.

The problem I do have is that there is so very little water. Along with everything else, I am always thirsty. I dream of flowing rivers, cascading waterfalls, smooth placid lakes. And I have terrible dreams about water, too—rushing to the shore of a gorgeous lake set majestically amidst lush green mountains and splashing into it, ducking down my head and taking a huge mouthful only to discover that the water is not only salt but unbelievably salt, so salt-thick that it burns my mouth and tongue and I awaken choking, gasping, spitting.

I would like to parcel out my water—there isn't much, I think the plastic carafe is only a little bigger than a soda can—but I quickly learned this isn't possible here. Once, when I determinedly left half my water for later, I eventually fell asleep—and upon waking discovered all the dinner things gone, including the half-full carafe. How I screamed then! How hysterical I was!

But I learned, too. Whatever is given must be devoured or used immediately, lest it vanish.

4. How I Came Here

I will remember this. I'll remember it all. I must. Over and over, again and again I'll repeat the words until they're tattooed into my blood, my bones, my DNA. Words, sentences, paragraphs spinning invisibly around in my head and yet locked down tight in a special room of memory reserved just for the purpose....

I have it all now, firmly. I've gone over it all hundreds of times. I know it as surely as a fine Shakespearean actor knows his Othello, his Macbeth, his Lear.

It may be weeks since I began this invisible document, my journal of the mind. It may be months. I don't know. But in thinking about what I've created I've realized that this record needs some background, some context.

Anyone reading this (as if that were possible) would naturally want to know who I am. It's a good question, as I sometimes have trouble remembering. For some reason, trivia is quite clear in my mind. I can remember every scene and most lines of dialogue from some films, every song— every verse, every chorus, every instrumental bridge—from some albums. It's the important memories which seem to have disappeared.

Yet I do remember things. I was married, I had a job, we lived in the city. In a house. I'm sure it was in a house. I had children, two of them, two girls—I think—and when I was first here that was perhaps my main thought, again and again: What about the kids? But my husband is taking care of them, I'm sure. The longer I've stayed here, the more abstracted they are in my mind—the children and my husband both. As if reincarnation is true, which I don't believe, and what I remember of them is from some other life, through a hazy gauze of half-memory. The problem with being here is that after a time it becomes difficult to know what is real in one's memories and what is simply fantasy. I remember my husband—I even think I can picture his face, red, ruddy, the kind of face that belongs to a man who spends a great deal of time outdoors, yet handsome for all that. And, yes, he worked with the forestry service, I'm sure I remember. When we met, I—an urban child—had never so much as camped overnight. He introduced me to a whole new world, a world of nature, black oak trees and spruces and white pines, of animals, of birds. I was amazed to realize after a few years that my city-dwelling self now actually knew the difference between, say, starlings and grackles, or red-bellied woodpeckers and downy ones.

Yes, I'm sure I recall all that. I'm sure it's real.

Anyway, the question naturally arises of how I came to be here.

The problem, as with everything else, is that I don't know. I have no clear last memory of life elsewhere, above ground, in the sunlight. I don't have any idea if I was drugged and kidnapped in my sleep, or grabbed bodily off the sidewalk and thrown into a waiting vehicle, or beaten into submission in some back alley and carried to this place. I simply don't know. One day ("day") I was here, that's all.

5. Possible Motives for My Being Here

Of course I've spent a great deal of time thinking about this topic. But again, it's impossible for me to know. Somewhere in my mind exists a thread that tells me there was political trouble where we lived, it was dangerous, the ruling party had cracked down on dissidents and thugs roamed the streets beating and imprisoning people. But was I a dissident? What was I dissenting from? And is this a memory from life or a memory from a news article, a movie?

I sense that at one point I knew the answers, but at times I find that the more I try to think, the more confused I become. It's when I'm *not* thinking of a thing that I find it can suddenly pop into my head—vividly, unquestionably, like my husband's face, which I'm quite sure is real. Or was.

I wonder too about individuals' motives. My husband? I can see his face screwing up in anger, I can see him yelling at me, at the children. At least I think that I can see this. Would he have put me here? Why? How could he have found such a place, a brick-and-cement cylinder drilled deep into the ground? Could he have had it built? Could it have been an existing structure, like a well? (No, it's too wide for any well.) And if it was my husband, how is he feeding me, how is he keeping other people from knowing?

Is it possible they—whoever "they" may be—took him, too? And the kids? That we're all in places like this, that there is an entire system of them underground, thousands of black cylinders holding thousands of bewildered people?

There was a boyfriend. Once upon a time. But was that during the marriage? It seems to me it must have been before, long before. But I don't know. Am I an adulteress? Have I been sentenced to imprisonment for the crime of adultery? There was a boyfriend, I can see him, young, sandy-haired, I remember lying under him with my legs wide in a narrow bed which seemed cramped and uncomfortable then but now would be a bed for royalty, a bed for the gods. The words *dorm room* come to mind, but was that where I was with him? Was he a college boyfriend? Or have I confused this with someone else, something else? Did it happen at all?

Or am I the victim of a random crime, some maniac who chose me simply because I was there? But such people torture, such people rape. For that to happen he would have to come in here, he would have to grab me and punch my face and tear at my skin and throw me down onto the cement and hold his hand over my mouth as he rammed his hard penis into me and fucked me until I bled, until I passed out from the pain and terror. Yet he's done nothing of the sort. I wish he would. I wish that very much. It would bring a certain clarity.

6. Ways to Die

Some time has passed. I don't know how much. And yet I believe I recall my entire journal, word-for-word. I have a disciplined mind and an excellent memory for such things. My numbers and titles help. *1. A Beginning, 2. Where I Live, 3. How I Live, 4. How I Came Here, 5. Possible Motives for My Being Here,* and now *6. Ways to Die.* When I recall the title I then work on the first words, *I will remember this, It would be tempting to say, One illusion I allow myself, I will remember this* again, *Of course I've spent a great deal of time thinking,* and the new *Some time has passed.* Once I have the title and the first line the rest comes easily, through simple mental discipline. I can even recite the sections—silently or aloud—in different order, in any order. When I escape here or when someone lets me out the first thing I'll do after embracing my husband and children is demand a computer or typewriter or pen and paper and write all this down so that it doesn't just vanish when my brain does. A recorder would help, a tape recorder. I could dictate the entire document and then type it up at my leisure. Yes.

I believe it's possible I tried to kill myself. I have a rather horrible abrasion which could only have come from ramming my forehead into the wall, perhaps repeatedly. As I've said, I have done this before, yet I'm disappointed with myself as I thought I'd gotten past such things. I have a husband, I have two daughters, I must survive this for them. For it *is* survivable. The fact that this place exists, the fact that I am fed and given a pot to use as a toilet means that people know about this. Certainly at the very least, one does. But probably more. And I must be missed. People know I'm gone, which means people are looking for me. I may be the object of a huge search, hundreds of volunteers spreading out through city streets and over green fields with the belief that at any moment they may discover my desiccated corpse. There must be leads. There must be people who saw me on my last day. They must have constructed a timeline, studied my movements on that last day, in those final hours. They must have theories. They may even have suspects. Those suspects may even be the right ones, and at any moment a blinding shaft of light may appear from above and I may hear a voice, probably a man's, calling out, *Is there anyone down there?* And I must be ready for such a moment, even if the light burns out my retinas forever. I must be prepared to call out *I'm here, I'm here, save me!*

I've spent a long time mediating on the topic of "Ways to Die." It's surprisingly difficult, I've found, to kill yourself by slamming your head against a wall. I've tried it again and again; apparently I tried it recently. The problem is that one collapses in pain or unconsciousness before death is achieved. The only real way, I suppose, would be a single blow so hard that dying would be instantaneous. So far I've been unable to manage that.

There is also wounding oneself in other ways. I seem to remember that out in the wilderness a fox or wolf caught in a trap will chew off its own leg in order to be free. Could I chew off my own leg? Unlikely, but I think I recall a story somewhere of a man who cut off his own arm in order to escape some trap. But he must have had a knife or at least some sharp instrument. Could I open a wound so big on myself that I would bleed to death? I suppose it's possible, but I would have to do it with my teeth. And my teeth are in poor condition, loose and wobbly in my gums.

There is the hunger strike. I could simply refuse to eat. Thus far I've been unable to do that, so ravenous by the time that food arrives and so terrified that it will be taken away that I simply devour it all immediately.

Could I poison myself? I can't think how I would do it unless I used my own piss and shit, and I don't believe I produce enough of either to kill myself. I could certainly make myself violently ill, but actual death seems unlikely. Every time the pot is brought back it has been emptied—not cleaned, but emptied. There's no build-up. No, I'm sure there wouldn't be enough.

And so I'll go on living.

7. Feelings

There are times when what I feel seems exceedingly strange—to the point that I wonder if my food may be drugged. The feeling may not seem strange at the moment I have it, but later, upon reflection, I wonder how I could have thought such a thing. I had such a feeling recently. The feeling came when I realized that my dinner had been delivered. I was delighted at this realization. I was hungry, I was thirsty, and now I would be satisfied. Moreover, I hadn't messed the floor since the last dinner, and so I would be able to use my toilet with some shred of dignity. In fact, that is the first thing I did.

As I ate my dinner I began to think about the person who delivers these things to me. I was convinced it was a man, though I don't know why. It could be a woman, it could be a child, it could be a revolving group of people. But I don't think it is. My fingers tell me that things are always arranged on the tray in exactly the same manner, which suggests the same person doing it. Of course a different person could be delivering the tray than preparing the food, but again, I don't believe this. I believe that one person is responsible for my eating, drinking, and excretory needs, and I believe that this person is a man. I pictured his hands, one holding the plastic plate, the other a ladle dipping into a pot of gruel. I pictured him searching the pot for the very best morsels, the biggest carrot shavings, the meatiest bits of gristle, trying to make my meal as much a proper repast as he could. I pictured him topping up the carafe of water to the very brim, to make sure I received as much as possible. Why didn't he do more? Why didn't he give me proper food, a huge pitcher of water? Because he was powerless, of course, under threat himself, as in a prison camp where some inmates get certain privileges which can be quickly snatched away. He wanted to, I realized. He wanted to help me. He was doing what he could.

And I loved him for it.

The feeling was overwhelming, undeniable. The faceless, nameless stranger who delivered gruel and water and a dirty plastic chamber pot to me suddenly seemed the most wonderful person in the world, the most kind, the most generous. I wanted to see him, gaze into his eyes, enfold him in my arms. I crawled around on my knees, whispering to him at the place where the wall joins the floor: "I know what you're trying to do, I appreciate it so much, I love you, I love you, I love you." Again and again, circling the black cylinder, convinced that if I kept whispering it—I couldn't shout it, he might get in trouble—that he would surely hear it, was hearing it even now, was grief-stricken that he could not help me more and yet happy that I recognized his efforts and how dangerous they were for him. I couldn't really picture the man in my mind except that he was slender, graceful, with beautiful hands, the most beautiful hands in the world. But that was all I needed to see. ("See.") He was there and he was on my side and he was working to help me. He wanted to help me stay strong. He wanted to help me escape. We would escape together, I would hear a panel shushing open in the darkness and hear a whispered voice, *It's time, come, you have to come now!* And off we would run. I pictured us in a dark forest, the sound of little living things everywhere around. Behind us, they were chasing us, we must run, run, my hand in this wonderful man's, as we made our escape.

This was all wonderful to think of but also, I recognize, a bit odd. Reflecting on it now I realize that I should most likely not idolize my captor, who after all may be nothing like what I've imagined. It could be that there is plenty of food available where he is and that there is no restriction on anything he gives me, that he could supply me with elegant three-course meals five times a day if he wanted, he could provide me with huge pitchers of water and bottles of wine, he could install lights and a flush toilet in here, he could...

He could let me out.

Surely it would not be difficult. Surely there is a door somewhere. He must have access to this place, else how did I get in here? A door, a panel, a window somewhere up out of my reach. How can he place the tray in here again and again, over weeks and months, knowing there is a sick, defenseless woman in here, and not do something about it? Whether he's working for himself or for others, he's a sadist, a psychopath. He must be. He enjoys the idea of my suffering, enjoys keeping me in darkness, laughs at the idea of taking away my toilet and making me either hold it until I'm in agony or piss all over the floor, grins at the thought of me reduced to licking the cold gruel from the plastic plate. And what kind of enjoyment does all this bring him? It would make more sense if there were at least a little light in here, enough that he could look down through his one-way window or whatever, and delight in watching my naked body writhe on the floor, chuckle as I hurl myself against the wall. Yet surely he can't see any more than I can in here, which is nothing at all. Who does this? What kind of monster?

I hate him. I hate him with a sharp deadly hatred that could cut diamonds, melt steel. My hatred radiates throughout this dark cylinder until I feel I almost generate my own terrible light, a sick red despising glow. I shout at him about his cowardice, his pitiful weakness. In my rage I grow quite vulgar. "Is it because you can't fuck a woman? Is that why you put me here? Because your dick won't stay hard when you try to stick it into a woman? Are you scared of girls? Are you scared of our *pussies?* Is that what's wrong with you?" I'm screaming, something I don't like to do, but somehow I must. How I wish I could hear an answer, any answer. A door shutting far away. A whisper of breeze. A deep distant voice chuckling, "Eat shit, bitch." But there's nothing.

8. An Interesting Development

I've been working my finger around the crack in the floor lately and I've become convinced that it is longer than it used to be. Longer and somewhat wider. Not wide, mind you—it's not like the change is anything dramatic—but it *is* change, and so I've been picking at it, slowly, carefully, and I think that I'm making progress. Progress toward what, of course, is the question. What might be underneath this place? Probably just dirt and rock. But if I could get there, if I could open the crack wide enough to fit my body through I could tunnel like a mole through the dirt and find my way up into sunlight again. *Something* must be there under the crack. This place wasn't built on top of nothing.

I'll keep working at it.

9. Progress

In my interest in the crack in the floor I've neglected my journal-study. I can feel it. My mind is having a tougher time recalling all portions of this journal and it's taken me quite some time to rebuild what was becoming a somewhat crumbling edifice. I think I have it back again, but it was not easy. At first I couldn't even recall the section titles. But once I had each one back in sequence I was able to build the first sentences and then the rest. I must not allow my excitement at the prospect of what is under this floor to destroy the one thing I have, the one thing they can't take away, which is this journal.

But I have made great progress! The crack is longer now, at least a foot long, and wider—I can actually stick the tip of my little finger into it as far as perhaps a quarter-inch. The crack *is* growing. Is the man who feeds me, the man I love, helping this along somehow? Will he at some point push open the crack from below, put his head in and say, "Close your eyes, I don't want to blind you, I'm busting this floor open and we're going together now, you're free"? Or is it the man who hates me, the one who's scared of women, the one who deliberately holds me here simply because he enjoys it? Because I've come to wonder if there mightn't be *two* people who care for me, one loving and kind, the other hateful. Are they engaged in some sort of battle over me? What is their connection? Are they father and son? Brothers? Is one caring and sweet, beautiful, gentle, while the other is a raging animal, ugly, destructive? Are they fighting over me even now, somewhere that I can't see or hear, are they engaged in terrible shouting matches, physical struggles? Will my love emerge victorious? Will he save me?

Of course it's quite possible that this is madness, that there are no brothers. It's difficult to recall sometimes that I don't actually *know* anything. That my situation hasn't really changed since the first day or night I was brought here, when I woke into the dark and became hysterical and started screaming a scream that didn't end for a very long time.

Maybe it still hasn't.

10. Further Progress

It's happening—it really is!

Nothing has changed, whatever time has gone by, and I think it may be a long time. The darkness is impenetrable and forever. The food and water and chamber pot come and they go. I know nothing, learn nothing. I shiver, I hold myself against the cold.

But now I have a project, a goal! The crack is definitely wider now, much longer and wider than it was before. I don't know why. Perhaps when this torture chamber was built— and it could be very old, after all—the foundation wasn't laid correctly. Maybe there is no foundation at all, just a crudely laid slab of concrete that has inevitably begun to break apart over time. Whatever it is, the crack is quite pronounced now. Sometimes when I lean down and press my ear to it I almost believe I can hear it growing, snaking out across the floor, a kind of grating sound. And when I dig at it with my fingertips

I make real progress, significant bits of concrete coming off onto my hands. There are enough such bits that I've begun a little pile of them in one corner. There isn't much now, maybe it all adds up to no more than a very small anthill, but it's there and it's growing all the time because I keep working at it. Over time, of course, my fingers tear and bleed and so I switch to other fingers. My ring finger and pinkies have gotten surprisingly good at scraping away at hard concrete. And while I do this I run over my journal again and again, the words solid and real in my mind the way little of anything else is. I cannot remember the names of my daughters (am I sure I have children?) but I remember every word of my brain-journal. Ten sections so far, starting with "1. A Beginning" ("I will remember this...") and now "10. Further Progress" ("It's happening—it really is!"), which itself is in-progress.

I must not allow the confusions of my memory to get in the way of my goals. The first goal, the most important, is to get out of here. The way I will do that is by tunneling down through the concrete and then up again into the light. The second goal is to hold onto my journal, all the words of it. This I will do by repeating, repeating, repeating, just as I'm doing now. The rest can be held for later. My children's names. My husband. Where I lived. None of it matters now. It will matter again in the future, but for now I must focus all my energy and all my strength on my two goals. There can be nothing else for me. I'm happier at this moment than I have been in a very, very long time!

11. Later

I have been sick. Really very sick. I remember throwing up many times and even now there are bits of vomit in what remains of my hair. In idle moments I try to pick them out. They are dry and easy to find and toss away. I believe I may have been delirious for a time. I think what happened is that I allowed my mind to wander off in unproductive directions, in thinking about who I am, why I'm here, how anyone could torment another human being in this way, and if it is really possible that I will never escape at all, that I will simply die here without explanation, without answers. That seems quite intolerable to me. The darkness seems intolerable to me. I would sell my body, whatever is left of it, for a glimpse of light, any light. And I would sell my soul, whatever is left of it, for the sound of a human voice, even one screaming at me calling me a filthy cunt. *Anything.*

No. I must not go off in such directions. I will keep those words simply as a further memorization exercise, but they'll have no meaning to me. I can't let them.

I must focus. I have lost valuable tunneling time. My little pile of concrete bits is still there, disappointingly small but quite real. I add to it all the time though it's difficult with my fingers scraped as raw as they are. I've even tried using my toes but that doesn't work. I also considered tearing off part of one of the pieces used to deliver my food, water, and toilet, but the plastic is too strong for me to rip. (I also feared the repercussions of someone discovering a bit missing from one of the items—perhaps no more food or water for a long time, no more chamber pot.) So I just have to keep digging, ignoring the pain, using the words of this brain-journal to strengthen me. And they do strengthen me. This journal is who I am, the words indistinguishable from myself. I must never lose it, never through inattention allow it to fade from my mind. For the words to crumble away would be the same as me crumbling away to nothingness. It cannot happen.

12. More Sickness

I've been sick again. For a long time. It is so dark here. I don't know how much longer I can do this. I'm very cold. Please let me out. Please let me out. Please let me out. *Please let me out.*

13. Recovering

I fear the quality of this journal has been low lately, though I've tried to keep it going. More importantly, I've tried to make sure that all the words remain intact. And they do. I'm sure that there have been twelve chapters, with the thirteenth in-progress. It gives me great comfort to know this. I feel better now and I keep digging, keep digging.

14. Success!

I can see through the crack now! For the first time since I came to this place, I witnessed with my own eyes an infinitesimal thread of light coming from one small bit of the crack. The crack is much wider than it was. I have been working on it all the time, for what seems like forever. Years. I feel that I am old now. But I will escape!

I'm careful. It's tempting, of course, to scream into the little hole with its dull thread of light—more like a hint of a thread, a ghost of one—to scream for someone, anyone, to save me. But it's possible that *they* would hear, whoever holds me in this place, whether the bad man or an entire league of bad men. I must stay quiet, must bide my time. Scrape. Scratch. Dig.

15. An End

This will be the final entry of my journal of the brain.

I remember it all, even now. I know I've gone through periods when my mind wasn't clear, when I gave up hope and only dreamed of dying, of being dead. But I was always able to come back to this journal, all fourteen-and-now-fifteen sections of it, my words, my soul.

The journal will end now.

It will end because the crack is now very large, the pile of cement rubble beside it huge. I can see it all now. I am no longer in the darkness. Light pours up from the place beneath me, bathing me in it.

Nothing has changed otherwise. The food still arrives, though I can hardly bear to eat it now that I can *see* it. The water arrives in the little carafe. The chamber pot. All of these items, by the way, are dark blue in color. And I was right about the cylindrical walls of this room—they are glossily painted brick. Black. The floor is plain gray cement, stained everywhere with my piss and shit and blood.

But in the middle of the floor is my salvation! The crack finally began to give easily, and I was able to start pulling away chunks of floor as big as the tip of my finger. Soon I had enough torn away to be able to reach my whole hand in. Eventually I cleared enough that I think, with some effort, I will be able to drop my body through.

But I know I must be careful, and so I am sitting here staring down into the lighted hole and remembering, for the last time, these last words of my journal of the brain.

There isn't much left of me. Looking at myself in the pale yellow light I see I'm utterly emaciated, my stomach contracted, my ribs outlined hard and prominent against my skin. My hands, ropy and desiccated, are covered in violent sores and pustules. There is little left of any of my fingertips. The nails are gone.

I'm filthy, of course. Covered with gray and brown stains, red and purple bruises.

I will describe what I see in the light below me.

It's a dim, golden-tinged world in what appears to be a huge cavern. There are shapes everywhere, manufactured shapes of things I cannot truly describe. The shapes are strangely geometrical and made of substances I can't identify. On the walls are splashed colorful pictures of unusual beasts, monsters with what appear to be slippery, slimy bodies, a bit like huge eels with the heads of something like horses.

The cavern is occupied. Darting here and there I see large furry creatures, brown and black, with long tails and hands or paws which appear to have cups on the ends rather than claws. They use these cups for suction when they climb the walls. The eyes of these beings are huge, wide-staring, a bit like the eyes of lemurs. When they talk, as they seem to, they do so with high-pitched chittering sounds.

The light in their chamber is a pale yellow. I've never seen a light quite like it. I do not know where it comes from.

Are these creatures my jailers? Will they kill me when they detect my presence? Will they eat me?

Or are they prisoners as well?

I am about to find out.

Once upon a time I was a wife, a mother. I lived in another place. Now...

I will remember this. I'll remember it all. I must.

On Tuesday the Stars All Fell From the Sky

◯◯◯

When Terrence Stillwater woke that morning in the pre-dawn dark he knew it was time. He had no idea *how* he knew, but he was as certain of it as he was that the sun rose in the east and set in the west and that the stars came out at night. Without hesitation he placed his bare feet on the floor and reached to the night table where, some months earlier, and unknown to anyone else, he had placed a Smith and Wesson 9 mm Sigma pistol in a drawer under a stack of magazines. The gun, for which he had a legal permit, was fully loaded. He was not an experienced marksman, having had only a single one-hour lesson at the nearby firing range shortly after he purchased the weapon, but he knew all he needed.

He stood with the gun in his right hand. He was wearing his old blue pajamas, the ones Kirsten had said jokingly for years he should for-God's-sake throw away; there were holes in both elbows of the shirt, and the pants were frayed at the ends, loose threads drooping out everywhere. But they were comfortable and he liked them. He inhaled in the darkness of the bedroom and listened to his wife's slow, even breathing behind him, feeling oddly disconnected from himself—as if he were not only the man people called Terry Stillwater but also a nameless Other floating somewhere near the ceiling, looking dispassionately down at the scene. Not that there was much unusual to see: a middle-class couple's dim bedroom, the pretty blonde wife asleep on her side with a floral bedcover up to her shoulders, and the tall, gaunt husband standing facing away from her on the other side of the bed. It might have been a scene painted by Edward Hopper or Grant Wood, except for the black 9mm pistol in the husband's right hand.

He turned and picked up his pillow with his free hand. Then he stepped around the bed to his wife and, after making sure the safety was off and the gun was ready to fire, he leaned down and covered the side of her head with the pillow, drew the weapon up quickly, and squeezed the trigger.

He was startled at how much sound the gun produced, even muffled by the pillow; he reflexively glanced up, as if someone might come running into the room. But the house was silent. Looking down again he realized he was still pressing the pillow to his wife's head and he stepped back, let it go. Dark blood bloomed around the blackened hole in the pillow, but she didn't move, made no sound. Her body might have jerked at the instant he fired—the part of him floating near the ceiling thought he'd seen this—but he wasn't sure. Already the moment was blurred in his memory, like a dream or fantasy of something that had never really happened.

He stood looking down at her, but there was nothing to see. Her arm was out before her just as it had been before. He could see the silver wedding ring on her third finger. For all the world it was as if he could simply take the pillow away from her head and say, "Honey? Have you had an accident? Your head is bleeding," and she would wake groggily, feel her temple, see the blood come away on her fingertips, say, "Gosh, I must have hit it on something, that's weird," and she would stand and move to the bathroom, switch on the light, run water and splash it on the side of her head, say, "Wow, I have no idea what this is, but don't worry, Terry, I'm fine, it washes right out. I must have cut myself somehow."

He did not remove the pillow. He stood there for a long time. Then he turned and walked into the hall which was covered by the green shag carpet he had always disliked. The first door on the left was Jodie's room. He turned the handle of the door softly. It was a typical thirteen-year-old girl's room, posters of boy bands on the walls and a great deal of splayed mess everywhere—clothes, stuffed animals, schoolbooks, papers. The room was suffused in a sickly yellow glow from a Donald Duck nightlight she insisted on keeping plugged into the wall. Jodie often had trouble falling asleep, though once she did she could sleep for twelve hours straight.

She was lying on her stomach, her short blonde hair awry, her head dangling partly over the edge of the bed. It looked like an extraordinarily uncomfortable way to sleep. Most of her bedclothes had been pushed off. She was wearing her big yellow smiley-face nightshirt. Stillwater took one of the bed's decorative pillows that had fallen to the floor and placed it against the back of his daughter's head, then fired the gun. This time it was different than with his wife. Jodie's head bucked severely, causing him to lose the grip on the pillow. It tumbled away. Blood poured out from the black wound in her skull, spraying her hair and the bed sheets. Her body jerked violently again and again and a sound seemed to come from deep in her throat, a confused growling. Her teeth chattered as if she were freezing. He took the bloody pillow up again, stood watching, suddenly frightened. He could feel his pulse charging. His breath was short. When she had more or less stopped moving he placed the pillow over the back of her head again and held it there for a time. Finally she was still.

He was nauseous now, his stomach threatening to come up through his throat. He tried to slow his breathing but it was hopeless. He was practically hyperventilating. He swallowed hard, shook his head, turned and marched fiercely up to Nelson's room at the end of the hall. He opened the door. In the semi-dark he could see the fifteen-year-old just starting to sit up in bed. "Dad?" he said groggily. "What's going on?" Stillwater raised the pistol and fired, the unmuffled sound deafening in the small room. Nelson's head crashed back against the wall behind him, leaving a huge dark spatter, and then, sighing shallowly, he fell gently down onto his side in the bed. He did not move again.

Stillwater found himself trembling. He left Nelson's room and moved back toward his own, his and Kirsten's. As he passed Jodie's room he saw—he could not help but see—that she had moved, that she was moving. It could not be, but it was. She had fallen out of the bed and was crawling on her stomach, so slowly and feebly that she was hardly in motion at all, toward her closet. The strange growling sound still issued from her throat. He tried to control his breathing, tried to calm himself. He walked up to where the quivering blood-drenched girl in her blood-drenched smiley-face nightshirt was trying to pull herself along with her hands. As he grabbed a pillow her head turned slightly and she looked up at him with blood running into her eyes and an expression he could not possibly describe and then he pushed the pillow onto her head and fired once more and she was still.

He walked back to his and his wife's bedroom. She had not moved. He placed the gun—the barrel was hot, he noticed—back into the drawer and covered it over with the magazines. Then he walked to the bathroom, flipped up the light switch. He looked perfectly normal, his expression the usual early-morning weary, his favorite blue pajamas just as they had been. He removed them slowly, staring at himself in the big bathroom mirror. He was a reasonably well-preserved example of a forty-three-year-old man. His jawline sagged a bit but his body had not run to fat. He was lean; that was what came from tennis three times a week and watching what he ate. It took discipline, that was all. Self-control.

He plugged in the electric razor and ran it over his face. When he was finished he turned on the shower, let the water grow warm, and then stepped in. It was only in the instant before the streaming spray hit his feet that he realized there were blood spatters on them. They melted and vanished in the water.

After carefully soaping and rinsing he turned off the spray and dried himself with his usual towel, the one that resided just to the right of his wife's on the rack. He replaced the towel, brushed his hair—it was a good, full head of hair, just turning silver at the sides—and applied underarm deodorant. Then he went to the bedroom and dressed: tidy powder-blue shirt, conservative tie, Khakis, comfortable old black loafers.

When he got to the kitchen he saw that the automatic coffee maker had completed its daily pre-timed pot and he poured himself a cup, adding sugar and cream. He placed bread in the toaster and when it popped out he buttered it. He took a green apple from the bowl and sat at the kitchen counter eating his breakfast. It tasted good. When he was finished he put the cup and plate in the dishwasher. He moved to the front door, picking up his briefcase from the hallway as he moved. He placed it down again to slip on a light jacket—it was early fall, chilly in the mornings. He was about to pick up the briefcase again and step out when he realized that he had forgotten to take his multi-vitamin. He stepped back to the kitchen, took a pill from the bottle, cupped water in his palm from the sink, and swallowed the tablet with the water. He wiped his hand on the dishrag and moved to the front door, picking up the briefcase. Then he went to work.

◙◙◙

When he arrived in the faculty room he saw a yellow Post-It Note stuck to the side of his mailbox: *Please see me this morning. Ron.* "Ron" was Ron Hunter, the principal, for whom Stillwater had worked for the past seven years. Ron was given to such notes, and as often as not they were good news at the Morning Light Academy, this feel-good private school in the Maryland suburbs; Ron had a habit of calling a teacher in just to praise him, to tell him the teacher how much he appreciated the time he'd spent with the Debate Club or how a parent had called to praise an assignment he'd given or just to talk. Ron loved to talk, in his office, about all things connected to the education of young people. Sometimes such talks could be stimulating; other times they dragged on to no apparent point, Stillwater finding himself wondering what unpleasant task Ron might be avoiding by keeping him so long.

But he knew as soon as he knocked gently on the open door that this was not a good-news talk. Ron looked up from his desk and when he saw Stillwater, frowned.

"Come in, Terry," he said, his voice neutral. "Shut the door, if you would."

He did, then made his way to the upholstered chair facing Ron's desk. The principal was a big bear of a man, carefully attired in a well-tailored dark blue business-formal suit that de-emphasized how overweight he was. He was around fifty, his long hair and beard salt-and-pepper.

"Sit down," he said.

Stillwater sat down in the chair.

"Terry, I hate to start your day with this," the principal began, "but there's a bit of a problem. I just got off the phone with Dora." That would be Dora Bennington, the mother of his student Meredith. In such a small school all the parents were known to all the teachers and first names were all that was needed.

Stillwater nodded uncomfortably. "I can guess what it was about."

"She said you 'popped off' at Meredith yesterday. Last period?"

He felt a trickle of perspiration run down his neck, but he knew how to handle the situation. "I did. We got into a bit of an argument. I let it get out of hand. It was totally my fault."

"What were you arguing about?"

He smiled weakly. "Personal responsibility, if you can believe it."

Ron smiled slightly, allowing the atmosphere in the room to ease a little. "Is she for it or against it?"

"Well, she said that if someone hired a worker who did a bad job then it was at least partly the employer's fault, for hiring the worker in the first place. I said that the worker's performance, barring any unusual circumstances, was entirely the worker's responsibility. It's the Ethics and Philosophy course, you know."

"Yes."

"Anyway, it was stupid on my part. When she dug in, I dug in. Classic teacher's mistake."

"And the 'popping off...?"

"I told her that her position was childish. Well, I said it in a raised voice. She got mad and went off to the bathroom.

When she came back a few minutes later she seemed fine, so I let it drop. I should have apologized to her."

"Will you do that today?"

"Sure. Of course."

"That will be fine. Send Dora an e-mail after you do, all right?"

"Yes. Glad to. I'm awfully sorry about it."

"No harm done, I'm sure." Ron smiled. Stillwater was about to stand when the principal went on: "Terry, are you suffering from any stress?"

"Hm?" He felt another line of perspiration trickle down his neck and his head began to throb lightly. Nothing too bad, just the very slight beginnings of a headache.

"Stress. Are you having any stress?"

"I—stress? I don't know. No more than any teacher, I guess."

"You've seemed stressed lately. I've missed your humor around here."

Stillwater tried to tamp down the anger he'd begun to feel. Leave it to Ron to butt into his business, into everyone's business. He did it all the time, seemingly feeling the need to not just be people's boss but their mentor, their guru.

"I—I don't know. I'm not aware..."

"You just haven't seemed very happy. When I walk by your classrooms I don't hear the kind of laughter I used to."

What the hell was he supposed to say to that? "I—maybe. Maybe a little stress, yeah."

"You're not thinking of leaving us, Terry, are you?"

"No. No, not at all."

"Good. You're far too valuable."

"No, I don't want to leave. I just...I don't know. Maybe you're right, maybe I'm suffering from some stress."

"Come on, Terry," he said, leaning forward, suddenly sympathetic. "You teach full-time, you've got two teenagers at home. Anybody would be stressed. How old are Nelson and Jodie now?" Ron never forgot the names of his staff's family.

"Fifteen. Nelson's fifteen. Jodie's thirteen."

"It's tough. I raised teenagers myself, you know."

"I know."

"Do you mind if I make a suggestion?" Ron's voice grew warm and friendly now. This was his classic bad-meeting approach: deal directly with the problem, switch the topic to a larger, related matter, and finish on a positive note with a prescription for the future.

"No, please, go ahead."

"Yoga." Ron nodded. "Terry, a few years ago Beth—" his wife—"turned me on to yoga. It's so freeing, so centering. I love it. Have you ever tried it?"

"No...no, I can't say that I have."

"It only takes an hour or two a week. To make a *huge* difference in your stress. They have yoga classes at the community center just down the street. That's where I go."

"Oh, good."

"You should give it a try. Works wonders."

"Maybe I'll do that. Thank you." Again he moved to stand.

"Where did I put that card?" Ron shifted papers around on his messy desk. "I have a business card from my instructor, my favorite. Melody. Lovely name, isn't it? She'll give you one beginner's session for free. Try it, Terry."

"I will."

"Ah!" He held up the card triumphantly. "Here it is!"

Stillwater took it in his hand. "I'll call. Thanks."

"Do it today," Ron said encouragingly. "So you don't forget. Tell her that Ron Hunter sent you and that you're interested in the free beginner's session."

"I will. Thanks. This is great."

Ron smiled widely, ending the meeting. "That's terrific, Terry. And be sure to get in touch with Dora after you've talked to Meredith, all right?"

"I definitely will. I won't forget."

"Fabulous. Have a great day, Terry."

Stillwater smiled and stepped out of the office.

◻◻◻

He thought of nothing in particular as he taught his morning classes, moving blandly through Composition 1 (always a slog), Reading Skills (also a slog), and finally Introduction to Existentialism, one of what the Morning Light Academy teachers referred to as a "goody" course, something a teacher invented himself and on which he was, in essence, the sole authority in school. He spent an enjoyable forty-five minutes with the brightest seniors discussing Camus.

"Camus writes about what he calls the absurd man," Stillwater said, pacing the classroom as he habitually did. "What is the absurd man?"

Nick Slate's hand shot up, as it always did for every question. Since it was the start of the period, Stillwater called on him, knowing he would have to avoid Nick's ever-eager hand later in the period lest the entire class become no more than a two-person discussion.

"A logical person in an illogical universe," the boy said proudly. He flipped back his blonde hair in the slightly effeminate way he had.

"Let's say rational, Nick, rather than logical. And what is it that makes this man absurd?"

This time there were several hands. He called on Sammie—Samantha Irving, a dark-featured, stringy girl who in another time would have been anyone's stereotype of a young spinster-librarian, round glasses and all. "It's that he *knows* the universe is irrational. That it doesn't have any meaning."

"That creates his conflict," big, athletic John Estes put in.

"Because he's rational himself, right. But the universe isn't. Very good, people. Hey, some of you in here have done your reading." He smiled. They were a good class, really, the best he had—high-level thinkers who would all go to good colleges next year. "Now let's take it a bit further: what did you get from Camus's saying that there may be such a thing as a responsible person, but there is no such thing as a guilty one?"

And they were off and running, more kids entering this impassioned daily Socratic-method lesson of theirs. It was fun, intellectual fun, a more organized and directed version of the late-night college bull sessions most of them would no doubt engage in over the next few years. He felt good leading it, challenging their assumptions, questioning their conclusions, always encouraging them to take their thinking deeper. He was, he knew, a good teacher.

But when lunch period came his mood darkened. Standing at his faculty mailbox, looking at the circulars from educational companies that had appeared in it, he remembered Kirsten in the bathroom that morning, with her strange head injury. *Don't worry, Terry, I'm fine, it washes right out. I must have cut myself somehow.* And the kids? They had stayed home today, but he had trouble recalling why. A bug going around, no doubt. Sometimes it felt as if his entire family was falling apart, they spent so little time together, he felt so distant from them. Kristen had grown remote and he suspected it was only the kids who kept her in the marriage now. Nelson and Jodie were preoccupied with their social lives, their friends and sports activities; they rarely had anything to say to their father unless they wanted money. He wondered if Kirsten was planning to leave him. He'd seen signs, or what he thought might be signs. Mysterious phone calls that she would quickly hang up on when he entered the room. He thought about it as he moved to the staff refrigerator for his lunch, then realized that he'd forgotten to pack one that morning. Damn it—Kirsten hadn't done it for him, preoccupied with her head. He could visit the cafeteria, he supposed. But in the end he brushed past several other teachers ("Hey, Terry, how you doing?" "What's up, Terry?"), returned to his classroom, and locked the door behind him. It was a solid wood door, no glass in it at all. Then he went to the windows and, after smiling and waving at two girls from his Reading Skills class who happened to be passing by, he dropped the blinds. The room was semi-dark then. He was safe.

He sat at his desk and put his hands out onto it, palms down. He stayed there for a long time, not moving, feeling his heartbeat, listening to his breathing. Something he was wrong, he thought. He remembered then a terrible dream he'd had the night before, a dream of blood and violence, but who was in the dream or what was happening was murky to him now. He wondered if Kirsten was all right. He hoped so.

He hoped the cut on her head had proven to be superficial. But it must have been, he realized, because if it hadn't then he wouldn't have left the house, he wouldn't have gone to work. If something had been seriously wrong he would have driven her to the hospital or called 911 and waited there with her. That was what he would have done if there had been something seriously wrong. That made sense. That was rational. Yet as he sat there he found his breath coming fast and he began to feel light-headed, spacey. He should eat something, he knew, but he wasn't hungry. He should drink something. He should get up and move. But he continued to sit there, his hands—quivering now—in front of him on the desk. Kirsten didn't love him anymore. Nelson and Jodie didn't care about him. He knew all this, knew it with terrible certainty. He was afraid. Terribly afraid. His breathing grew faster and he heard a soft high-pitched whine coming from somewhere deep in his throat. He deserved more, he thought. More than this. He deserved happiness. He deserved love.

An explosion tore him from his reverie. But he realized instantly it wasn't an explosion. It was a knock at the door.

"Mr. Stillwater? Are you in there?" He recognized Victoria Norwood's voice. She was an exceptionally insecure sophomore who frequently asked for help with her essays during lunch period. He remained still, forcing his breathing to slow, his heartbeat to calm. He glanced at the classroom clock and realized that in twenty minutes he would have fifteen underclassmen in here and he would have to give them a quiz on the Hemingway story he'd assigned them for last night. Did he even have the questions ready? Yes, he realized, in his notebook. But he hadn't Xeroxed the sheet for them. He would have to do that. He *must* get control of himself.

Victoria knocked again. He knew if he waited she would give up and go away. He sat there, willing his bodily systems to slow down.

He did this for five minutes. Then he stood on unsteady legs and moved to turn on the light in the classroom. It seemed blinding, obscene. He allowed his eyes to adjust for a moment and then pulled open the classroom door, moving quickly into the central hall and out the front door. He marched away, off the campus, and turned onto a random side street containing a few small shops. Looking quickly around, he pulled out his cellphone and punched in the familiar number. It was suddenly desperately important to him that she pick up, *pick up.*

"Terry?"

Thank God. He swallowed, tried to talk, for a moment could not produce any sound. Finally he managed: "Hi...hi."

"What's up?" she asked, her voice carefully neutral. "Haven't heard from you in a while."

"I..."

After a moment: "Terry? Are you there?"

"Yes...yes."

"Is something wrong, amigo?"

"Angela, can we—can we get together this afternoon?"

"Get together? Why?" An edge crept into her voice.

"I—I'd just like to."

There was a long pause. He pictured her sitting at her drafting table in her office downtown, working on some big architectural sketch, the sunlight pouring over her shoulders and making her raven-black hair shine. She was thirty-two but looked younger, a small woman, thin, compactly built, dark-featured; when he'd first met her he'd thought she was Hispanic, which led forevermore to her teasingly calling him *amigo*. No, Angela Bart was Italian through and through, the original family name, Bartolomeo, having lost its last four syllables a hundred years before when her great-grandparents arrived in America. Angela was energetic and always on the go. She rarely wore jewelry or makeup; she didn't need them, really.

They'd been having an affair—well, *he* had, she wasn't married—for the past year, but it had sputtered out a month or so before. It hadn't officially ended. There had never been a moment when either of them said, *We have to stop doing this.* If Angela had felt guilty about betraying the grand sisterhood of females by getting involved with another woman's husband, she'd never let on. Stillwater himself felt no guilt about it at all. His marriage was nothing but a hollow husk waiting to be swept up and tossed in the trash. He suspected Kirsten had cheated on him more than once, though he couldn't prove it.

"Do we still get together, Terry? I didn't know."

"I'm sorry I haven't been in touch," he said, his voice low. "You know. Kirsten, the kids...a lot of..."

"You aren't just horny, are you, Terry?"

Just like Angela—straight to the point, no bullshit. He realized she must be alone in the office. *"No,"* he said emphatically. "It's...I just..."

"Terry, what's wrong? What is it?"

"I can't—can't talk. I have to get back to class. I just stepped out to call you."

"You don't sound good."

He couldn't think what to say to that.

"Okay," she said finally, with a little sigh. "When can you stop by?"

"When do you get home today?"

"Five or so. Want to make it six?"

"Six...yes, six. Let's make it six."

"What about your family?"

"They're out. They're gone. That's why I need to see you."

A pause. "And this isn't just sex, right?"

"It isn't just sex."

"Because if you show up with nothing but that on your mind you're going to go away disappointed."

"It isn't sex at all."

"Hm. I guess it isn't. Doesn't sound like it, anyway."

"It's not."

"I'll see you at six, Terry. We'll rustle up something to eat."

"That would be—" his voice was suddenly tight—"that would be great."

"Okay. Bye-bye."

"Bye," he whispered, but the line was already dead. He glanced at the phone and realized that he was nearly out of time. He rushed up the street again, brushed past numerous students as he made his way back to his classroom, found the sheet with the Hemingway quiz, and hustled quickly to the faculty room. He was nearly out of time and Sylvie Mercure, the lower-level Math teacher, was already at the Xerox machine. He shifted his weight from one foot to the other, cleared his throat.

"Well," she said, looking up and smiling, "is somebody in a hurry?"

"Please," he said, trying to return the smile. "It's just fifteen copies of one sheet. I need it this period."

"Oh, go ahead," she said, ever-indulgent. She was a nice woman. He thanked her, shoved the paper onto the glass, shut the top, and hit *Start*. Immediately the machine emitted a strange rasping noise and stopped working completely.

"Oop," said Sylvie. "Paper jam."

"Jam? What...?" He looked desperately from one part of the machine to another, opening and closing the little shelves and doors. His heart was pounding. Sweat poured from him. "I—I have to have this! I have to have it *now!*"

Sylvie Mercure looked at him oddly. "Okay, okay," she said. "Jeez, it's not the end of the world. I think the problem's down here." She popped open a panel he hadn't noticed and pulled a crumpled sheet of paper from it. Then she closed it again. "Try it now," she said.

He did. It worked perfectly. He watched nervously as the copies slid out of the mouth at the side of the machine, positive the thing would jam up again at any moment. When it didn't and his copies were finished, he looked sheepishly at Sylvie and said, "Sorry."

"Little tense, aren't you?"

He tried to laugh. "A little."

"It's only Tuesday, you know. Long way till Friday yet."

"Yes...I know. I'm sorry." He made his way to his classroom just before the bell rang. He smiled, he reminded them about the quiz, they groaned, he laughed. It went smoothly and easily; the quiz took most of the period, the discussion took the rest. Soon enough it was the last period of the day. He made it through that and as the bell rang, signaling the end of the school day, he asked Meredith Bennington to stay for a moment.

"Meredith, I'm sorry about yesterday," he said, standing by the door with her. "It was totally my fault."

"Oh, that?" she said casually, cocking her head. "It's okay, Mr. Stillwater, it's not that big a deal. I'm kind of pissy right now anyway. I'm on the rag."

He smiled and glanced away. "I think that comes under the heading of 'Too Much Information'."

She laughed. "Sorry!"

"So we're good?"

"Sure. You know you're my favorite teacher."

Actually he *hadn't* known that. "Well...okay, Meredith. Thanks."

"Bye, Mr. Stillwater!"

Then she was gone and he was alone in the classroom again.

Three-thirty. Two and a half hours.

He sat at his desk again and graded the quizzes mechanically, hardly reading what the students had written—instead just quickly locating key words in the answers that indicated they had the right idea. After he entered the scores into his grade book, he mulled over his lesson plans for Wednesday. He hadn't written down lesson plans in years, but he reviewed what he would do and made a mental inventory of any work he'd need to complete before then—any worksheets, any review reading, any videos. It was all simple enough. Wednesday would be a straightforward day for Mr. Stillwater, teacher.

He logged onto the classroom computer on his desk and typed out a brief e-mail to Meredith's mother: *Dora, Ron talked to me about your call and about what happened in class yesterday. I'm really sorry about it. It was all my fault, and Meredith had every right to be upset. It won't happen again. I spoke to Meredith just now and I think we're on good terms once more. Again, my apologies. Best, Terry Stillwater.* He hit "Send."

Then he sat there, staring at the computer screen, not moving. He sat there and he saw himself sitting there, from a vantage point near the ceiling: sweat poured from his face, his hands grew cold. He hoped Kirsten would be all right by the time he got home. She'd gotten a bad injury somehow and the blood had frightened him but she'd said, he knew she'd said, *Don't worry, Terry, I'm fine, it washes right out.* And the kids, were they all right? He'd left them in their bedrooms, not moving, not getting ready for school, but then again it had been early, still dark. But they'd been sick, sick with something. A virus, a bug. It had made them bleed, it was terrifying, but he was sure that they would be fine by the time he got home. When he got home he would ask Jodie about her math class, she struggled so in it, she had no head for numbers—such a cliché for girls, but true in her case—and maybe talk to Nelson about shooting some hoops in the driveway. And he should stop on the way home for ice cream—two kinds, something like chocolate chip or rocky road for everybody except Jodie, who loved pistachio, a flavor everyone else in the family hated. He would get her a container of pistachio.

Then he thought of Angela and realized that he would have to come up with an excuse so that he could leave around quarter of six to be with her. A meeting at school? He'd used that before. There was no school sporting event that he could visit for a few minutes and then leave, alas. It was difficult to think. Every time he tried to visualize telling Kirsten the lie his mind seemed to grow fuzzy, the image of her face fragmenting into pieces dropping away like bright-colored stars falling through the dark.

"Terry?"

His brain whipsawed back to the desk, the classroom, the face in the doorway. Ron Hunter, smiling.

"Yes, Ron."

"Called for the yoga yet?"

"No...I was just about to."

"Don't forget. It's important. Nothing like it for stress."

"Yes. I'm looking forward to trying it. Oh, and I talked to Meredith. And sent Dora an e-mail."

"Fantastic." Ron smiled and gave him a thumbs-up. "You're the best, Terry." With that textbook positive reinforcement, he wandered off.

Stillwater did not want to leave but he knew he couldn't stay here. He couldn't face any more interactions with students or faculty or—well, anybody. He stood suddenly, knocking his chair back against the wall. He felt extremely hot, yet the building was cool. He stuffed his various books and papers into the desk drawers and moved quickly to the door. At that moment, insecure little Victoria Norwood appeared with her books in her hand.

"Mr. Stillwater? I was wondering if you could help me with..."

"Tomorrow," he said, his voice a husky whisper. "Tomorrow." He pushed past her, rushed to the faculty room—thankfully empty—grabbed his briefcase and fled the building out the rear entrance.

◎◎◎

He drove aimlessly around town for a long while. The sky was beautiful in the late afternoon, deep autumn blue with billowing white clouds that made the sun appear and disappear. He wondered if he should stop to buy the ice cream. He wondered what he would say to Kirsten that could get him out of the house a little before six. He wondered if he should just call Angela back and say he couldn't make it after all. He felt jittery, as if little electrical pulses were popping up everywhere under his skin. At a stoplight he was jolted again by a horn from the car behind him; the light had switched to green and Terry hadn't even noticed. Son of a bitch, he thought. He checked his phone: nearly five. He had no choice; he would have to go home now.

He stopped at the little corner grocery a few blocks from the house and bought a large tub of chocolate chip ice cream and a pint of pistachio. When he brought the cash out of his pocket he fumbled it and the bills dropped to the counter and the change went skittering every which way. "God damn it," he muttered, "god damn it, god damn it." The clerk told him not to worry about it, she'd help him pick up the coins. With people behind him in the line he suddenly couldn't bear it, left a ten-dollar bill on the counter and fled with the ice cream containers in his hands.

Breathe, breathe. He tried to keep his pulse calm and steady as he pulled up in the driveway. Kirsten's car was still in the garage. He looked up and down the street as he got out of his vehicle; nothing unusual, a lovely day in the neighborhood. He took the mail from the box—nothing, just catalogs. He fumbled his keys as he reached the front door, then fumbled them a second time. He was shivering. Jesus Christ, he thought. Jesus Christ.

He opened the door.

The house was silent.

He did not call for his wife or his children. He said nothing at all. He walked in and closed the door behind him and hung his light jacket in the closet. He dropped the mail on the kitchen table. Then he walked to the refrigerator and brought out a beer, popped it open, and sat at the breakfast bar drinking it.

Now, none of this was real. He knew that. He knew perfectly well that none of it had happened. And yet he knew at the same time that it *had* happened, the thing his mind had successfully deflected all day but which had waited there malevolently, waited for him to come home and face it. He knew that it could not be true yet he knew that it was true. If, say, Jodie were to come bustling out of her bedroom with a bright, "Hi, Dad!" then it would not be true. But Jodie didn't do that. If Nelson were to come in through the back door and call out, "Dad, you want to play some one-on-one?" then it would not be true. But Nelson didn't do that, either. And if Kirsten called to him from the bedroom, said, "Honey, sorry I'm not getting up, I have a splitting headache," then it would not be true. But Kirsten didn't do that.

Nobody did anything. The house was still in the late-afternoon light.

He finished the beer.

Jodie liked pistachio. He was glad he'd remembered to buy some for her.

Because none of this had happened, he told himself. The fact that they were all silent indicated absolutely nothing. It was not *evidence.* They might all be out at the mall. Kirsten often took them there. They might have gone for a walk. They might be in three different places, for all he knew. They could be anywhere at all on planet Earth. There was nothing to say that they weren't.

He still hadn't managed to think of the excuse he was going to give Kirsten. He tried to come up with one. He hoped she didn't suddenly walk into the room before he was ready.

Kirsten's bag was on the counter next to him. He opened it and looked in. A billfold, lipstick, notepad, little container of tissues...and her little purple cellphone. He brought it out, flipped it open.

Two calls. He knew what they would be before he even brought them up on the screen: Jodie's school, Nelson's. Yes, there they were, the calls having come in within minutes of each other just past nine a.m. Both their schools were very good about contacting parents when their children were absent without a prearranged excuse.

He closed the phone slowly and set it on the counter. He stared at it for a moment.

Then he raised his fist and slammed it down on the instrument as hard as he could, caving it in, making a huge crack straight down the center. Tiny pieces skittered off along the counter and onto the floor.

His hand began to throb badly then, but he made no move to do anything about it. He just sat there with his fist tight on the counter and the pieces of the broken cellphone all around it.

Five-twenty.

Watching himself from the high place, he stood finally and walked to his and Kirsten's bedroom. The door was slightly ajar; he pushed it gently. He knew she would not be there, that there was no possibility she would be there. She was at the supermarket, at the library, she was picking up Jodie or Nelson somewhere or she was out at the little café where she sometimes went with a couple of her friends. She was at the doctor complaining about her headache.

She was on the bed, where he had left her. Her arm had not moved. The pillow was still over her head; it had soaked through over the past seven or eight hours and the room was suffused with a strange coppery odor; blood, he imagined. He considered the scene dispassionately. Something terribly violent had happened here, but it was as if it had happened to a stranger. He felt nothing about it. It was odd, that was all. Odd and inconvenient. He wouldn't mind talking with Kirsten just now, sharing a beer with her, hashing over the day.

He stepped out and up the hall to Jodie's room. Jodie was all right, he knew. She was a sturdy girl, a bright one. She would be excited to hear that he had brought home pistachio.

Jodie was on the floor, face down in her yellow smiley-face nightshirt, the pillow on her head. There was an extraordinary amount of blood everywhere, or at least he assumed it was blood—much of it appeared so dark that it might have been ink or tar. It was a much worse scene than with Kirsten. Standing in the doorway, he wondered why that might be. He wondered if the person lying there was even Jodie—she looked somehow bigger and heavier than he remembered her. As he breathed he smelled the distinct odor of urine and this bothered him—for God's sake, she'd been toilet-trained more than a decade ago, there was no excuse for this.

He closed the door and moved up to Nelson's room.

If Jodie didn't look like herself, Nelson hardly looked human at all. His forehead was gone, or rather scattered across the headboard and wall. This gave his head, which was not nearly as bloody as Stillwater might have imagined, a disturbing look, and he remembered suddenly, absurdly, what Emily Dickinson had said: *If I feel physically as if the top of my head were taken off, I know that is poetry.* Yet there was no poetry here. Where his head should have been there appeared to be some kind of pulpy gravy. Nelson's limbs were in strange, unnatural positions: the left arm uncomfortably under his body, the right dangling off into space, his left leg halfway off the bed and dangling near the floor. His T-shirt was hitched most of the way up his body, crumpled at weird angles, yet his shorts were perfectly arranged, utterly natural, as if he'd just slipped them on before his dad walked in. The odd coppery odor suffused this room, too.

He closed the door to Nelson's room and then made his way back to his own bedroom. He stripped off his tie and tossed it in the closet, then went into the bathroom and sat on the toilet in order to slip off his shoes. Standing again, he looked toward the bed. The sight bothered him. It annoyed it, made him angry. She had no right to be there like that, bothering him. He walked up to her and stared at the bare arm and outstretched hand with the wedding ring on the third finger. *Cut it out,* he wanted to say to her, *stop it right now.* Instead he took the comforter which had mostly fallen to the floor and threw it over her, covering her completely.

That was better.

As he was taking off his shirt some dark muscle seemed to cramp within his stomach and he rushed to the toilet again, this time raising the lid and getting on his knees and vomiting into it. He flushed, coughed, tried to clear his burning throat. His head throbbed. Finally he stood and turned to the bathroom counter. He reached to the medicine cabinet, found the bottle of ibuprofen there, poured half a dozen into his hand and swallowed them with huge handfuls of water.

He sat on the bed then, on the corner farthest from where Kirsten lay. He was shaking again. He wanted to lie down but no, that was impossible. Angela was expecting him. It occurred to him that he still had not thought of an excuse. He could write it on a Post-It Note, he thought, when he thought of it, and he could put it somewhere Kirsten was sure to see it when she woke up. On the refrigerator door, maybe.

Five twenty-five.

His phone bleeped in his pocket, causing him to jump up as if the bed were on fire. He flipped open the device, thinking it was probably Angela, but no: an unfamiliar name shone on the blue screen. "Soothe the Soul"? As he pressed the button and said "Hello?" it suddenly occurred to him that there was no reason for him to take this unknown call, but by then it was too late.

"Mr. Stillwater, please." A young, chirpy female voice.

"This is—this is Mr. Stillwater." His voice was a hollow whisper.

"Oh, great! Mr. Stillwater, this is Cathy from Soothe the Soul Yoga and Meditation. How are you today?"

"I'm...what do you want?"

"Mr. Stillwater, we got a call from your friend Ron Hunter, saying that you were interested in signing up to one of our free beginner's yoga sessions."

Jesus Christ. "Um...Yes. Sure."

"That's wonderful. We have an amazing beginning yoga instructor, Adele. Everyone raves about her. I'm sure you'll love her class."

A pause.

"Mr. Stillwater?"

"Yes...I'm here."

"When would you like to come in for your free class? Would evenings be better for you?"

"Evenings..."

"Well, there's a beginner's class on Thursday at 7:30 I could fit you into. Does that work for you?"

"Yes."

"Great. I'll put you down for it. You should wear comfortable clothes, Mr. Stillwater—sweats, if you have them. Anything loose that you can move freely in. Cotton is better than synthetics. And try not to eat anything too heavy before class."

"Yes. All right."

"Oh, and if you have to cancel for any reason, please let us know as far in advance as you can."

"I'll do that."

"So, we'll see you Thursday at 7:30!"

"Yes."

"Fantastic! Have a great day, Mr. Stillwater! Bye-bye!"

The line went dead.

He put the phone back in his pocket. Absurd, he thought.

The Absurd Man.

He changed into sweatshirt, blue jeans, and sneakers, leaving his work clothes scattered on the bed. He gathered a few extra clothes and toilet items and pushed them into an old brown book bag of his, then moved to the front room again.

Five-thirty. Late enough to head out.

Ignoring the shattered remnants of the cell phone on the counter (how had that gotten there?), he took a Post-It Note and scrawled on it, *Gone to soccer game at school.* It was lame—Kirsten would easily be able to find out that there was no soccer game if she checked—but it was all he could think of. He stuck the note to the handle of the refrigerator and stepped out, locking the door behind him. When he reached the car he tossed the book bag into the trunk and then dropped down into the driver's seat.

The ice cream was still sitting on the passenger seat next to him.

He looked at it for a long time. He should take it inside so that it wouldn't melt, he knew. But he didn't want to go back inside. He could take it to Angela, but she rarely ate sweets. Yet he needed to do *something.* He took the two containers in his hands and stared at them, suddenly hating them. They were a complication, a stupid complication like the idiotic yoga woman calling him. He had a sudden desire to smash both cartons, pummel them with his fists, but he held himself back. Self-control was important to him. He would not smash up the ice cream and get it all over the car and himself. He would not do it no matter how much he wanted to.

Finally he opened the window of the vehicle and tossed both containers onto the driveway. The smaller one, the pistachio, simply rolled to the edge of the grass and stopped. The other, the big one, lost its lid on impact and some of the ice cream sloshed onto the concrete. He didn't care. He didn't care at all. It no longer made any difference. He started the car and pulled out of the driveway, blasting his horn again and again though there was no one in sight.

◯◯◯

"Hey amigo," Angela said with a reserved smile when she opened the door to him.

"Hi." He tried to smile.

They briefly embraced, without passion or desire.

"C'mon in."

He stepped into the familiar apartment. Angela was a fussy housekeeper and the place was immaculate, carpet freshly vacuumed, books and magazines neatly shelved, everything in its place. Angela did not own a television, and this gave the main room an odd, unfocused quality, at least to his eyes—the sofa and leather chairs faced each other around the handsome glass coffee table instead of all facing the TV. It was not displeasing, only unusual.

"Drink?" she said.

"Yes. Sure."

He stood there awkwardly as he watched her move to the kitchen. She had not dressed up for him—he wouldn't have expected her to—nor was she wearing some easy to drop fuck-me thing like a half-open bathrobe. She had on her gray sweatpants and a loose pink T-shirt that advertised breast cancer awareness.

"I don't have any beer," she said from the refrigerator. "Wine?"

"Sure...wine's great."

She poured two glasses of Chardonnay and brought them back to the main room. Handing him one, she said, "Sit." He dropped down onto the sofa. She sat there as well, but on the other end. She tucked up her bare feet under her.

"What's up, Terry?" she said.

He sipped the wine. "I just—just wanted to see you."

"You've been pretty quiet lately. I didn't know where we stood."

"I'm sorry," he said, staring at the bland brown carpet. "I've been..."

"Busy, I know."

"Not busy." He shook his head and looked at her. "I'm sorry. I should have been in touch."

She shrugged, looking at her wine glass. "It's okay."

"No, I..." He sighed. "It hasn't been fair to you."

"I'll second that."

"I...I know."

They sat in silence for a time.

"How have you been?" she asked finally.

"Great." He nodded. Then: "Lousy."

"I'm sorry."

There was silence again.

"Are you interested in how *I've* been?" she said.

He glanced at her, then away. "Oh, God, Angela," he said, "I—of course I want to know how you've been. I'm—I keep saying I'm sorry, but I *am* sorry."

She scowled. "What's wrong?"

"I..." He inhaled, exhaled.

"What?"

"This was a mistake," he muttered finally, placing his wine glass on the table and standing. "I—this was a mistake. I'd better go."

She looked up at him. "If you think I'm going to jump up and throw my arms around you and beg you to stay, Terry, you're wrong."

"I know."

"You can go if you want." She tipped her head. "There's the door."

"I—know."

"But something's obviously bothering you. If you want to tell me about it, I'll listen."

He stared at the door for a moment, then sat again.

"Thank you," he said.

"Oh, Terry, knock this off. Just tell me whatever it is. If you're breaking up with me, don't worry about it. I half thought we were broken up anyway."

"No, it's not that. I—did something. Today."

"And what did you do?"

"I—my marriage is over."

She studied him. "What do you mean?"

"It's—over. It's over." Little flashes seemed to appear in front of his eyes and descend down the range of his vision until they vanished, like stars falling slowly through the dark.

"There are a lot of ways for a marriage to be over," she said musingly.

"She left," he said. "She's gone."

"Kirsten left? Left the house?"

"She left."

"What about Nelson and Jodie?"

"They're gone too."

She seemed to consider it, sipping her wine. "Where did they go?"

"I...I don't know. Maybe to her parents. I just—I only just found out. When I got home today."

She frowned. "You called me around lunchtime, though."

His mouth was dry. He took a swallow of wine. "Yes, that was..." He tried to think. "That was before I knew. But I'd seen...signs. I thought she would do this."

"But you don't know where they went? Kirsten didn't call you, or leave you a note?"

"No."

"Terry...are you sure they're all right? Something could have happened. Maybe this isn't what you think it is. I mean, God forbid."

"No, I..." He was trembling now. "No, she...she didn't leave a note, but she left...she...there was a Post-It Note. On the refrigerator door. On the handle."

"Then she *did* leave a note."

"Not really a note. Just...'Went to my mom's,' that's all it said."

"Well, how do you know she *left* you? Maybe..."

"No, they...they took their things. All their things. And I...I called. She—she wasn't there, but I—I called her mother. She said that Kirsten and the kids would be moving in with them for a while."

She looked at him carefully. "A minute ago you said you didn't know where she'd gone."

"I, Angela, I..." And it suddenly hit him, an overwhelming tidal wave of unnamable emotion. He started to cry, great hot tears flooding his cheeks. His gut clenched as if he would vomit, but he held it back. Angela's face softened as she watched him. But she didn't move.

"I'm just—confused," he said finally, in a hoarse whisper.

"I understand, Terry."

"It's—scary."

"I'm sure it is."

"It had to end," he said quietly, his voice rough. "I knew it. We both knew it. Kirsten and I. I'm just—the way it *happened*...I..."

After a while she said, "I'm sorry, Terry."

He inhaled shakily, nodded, finished his wine. "Any more of this?" he asked.

"Sure. But I don't want you getting drunk here."

"I'm not going to get drunk."

She looked at him, then stood and took his glass. "Okay."

As she moved around in the kitchen he tried to calm himself. He hated lying to her. Kirsten was waiting for him at home. He knew that. They'd just been out somewhere before. She would have started dinner by now. He should go home. But then he felt a silent jolt course through him. No, he did not want to go home. He couldn't. He couldn't go home ever again.

"Here." She held the glass out to him, not smiling. When she sat it was in the leather chair opposite the sofa.

"Thank you." He found a tissue in his pocket and blew his nose.

"So what are you going to do?" she asked after a while.

He shook his head. "I need to think."

"Yeah. I imagine." Her voice was not unkind.

"It's just that it's so sudden."

"Yeah."

"But..." He cleared his throat. "It *is* what I wanted."

"You sure?"

He nodded. "I've always cared about you, Angela."

"Terry, don't."

"I mean it."

"Don't start."

"I'm sorry, I just...I don't think you ever understood...it's just that with a wife and two kids and a job and..."

"I understand, Terry. I always did."

He looked at her. "It's different now. Everything's changed."

She didn't respond, looking at her wine glass.

"I mean," he began, "maybe..."

She looked at him quickly and stood. "Have you had dinner, Terry? Do you want something to eat?"

"Dinner? I..."

"Nothing much. I can see what's in the freezer. Some fish, maybe."

He wasn't hungry. He didn't believe he would ever be able to eat again in this world. He said, "That would be great. I'm starving."

◉◉◉

To Stillwater's surprise, he *was* starving. He wolfed down the broiled fish and broccoli as if it were hardly there at all and then went to work on the fruit on the table, plowing quickly through two apples, an orange, a banana.

"Good grief," Angela said, watching him while she picked away at her own food without interest. "When was the last time you ate something?"

"I—I don't remember," he said, his mouth full of apple.

"Well, take care of yourself," she said, finally pushing her plate away. "Do you want mine?"

"Sure." He pulled the plate to him, shoveled everything on it into his mouth in a few quick motions.

At last he sat back, stifling a burp. "Great," he said. "You were always a great cook."

She shrugged. "Just fish."

She got up and made tea while Stillwater sat back, feeling relaxed for the first time that day. In fact, he felt good. Life suddenly seemed very simple. His marriage was over. The future lay in front of him, a clear blue sky of possibilities.

They drank their tea quietly and then picked up the dishes together. They were practiced at this; Stillwater had had many a meal here when he was supposed to be somewhere else with Kirsten and the kids. But now he could do it without guilt, without shame. There was no more family in his life. He had no more family. There was something joyous about it.

She resisted slightly when he came up behind her at the sink and wrapped his arms around her. But only slightly. "Terry," she said, pushing him gently with her elbow, "cut it out."

He buried his face in her hair, fresh and lustrous. His hands moved and her protests quieted. She let him touch her. They didn't speak.

After a long time, and without looking at him, she took his hand and walked him back to her bedroom.

◯◯◯

"**D**on't worry about it, amigo," she said in the dark. "It happens. You've got a lot of stress."

"I don't feel like I'm stressed. Not anymore. Not now."

"Still."

They cuddled for a while, emotions roiling in him.

"Terry, maybe it's time…"

"Please don't make me leave," he said.

"Terry…"

"I can't go back there. Not to that house. Not tonight. Please."

◯◯◯

"**A**ngela?"

"Mm."

"Are you awake?"

"Mm…I am now."

"Let's go someplace."

"Hm?"

"I don't mean tonight. Tomorrow. Let's take a trip."

"What are you talking about, amigo?"

"Just a short one. I'll call in sick. Surely you can be away from the office for a day or two."

"Why? Where do you want to go?"

"I don't know. Just...away. The beach. The mountains. Somewhere."

"Oh, come on, Terry. Let me sleep."

"I'm serious. I—I've got to get away."

"Well, you don't need me for that."

"Of course I do. The two of us. Nothing between us anymore."

"Oh, be quiet."

"Will you? Go on a trip with me? Just for the day?"

She was silent for a moment. Then: "Well...I guess I could. I could call Susan tomorrow and tell her I won't be in. If I do that she'll know I'm with you, though. She always does. She thinks you're bad for me."

"I—I want to marry you, Angela."

"Don't say things like that."

"I do. I mean it."

"You're still married, you know. Just because Kirsten left...doesn't mean she won't come back."

"She won't come back, Angela."

"She might."

"No. She won't come back."

◯◯◯

A more beautiful autumn day he couldn't even have imagined. They drove up on long winding roads through the small towns and state forest parks of West Virginia, great American beech trees and yellow birches and black birches looming majestically on either side, endless groves of sugar maples spreading fiery seas of vivid red and gold before them, shadows from the bright sun casting chiaroscuro highlights over the scene. Stillwater drove easily, his breath calm and even, his mood relaxed. Much of the time his hand enfolded Angela's gently. She was smiling, he saw, looking genuinely happy for the first time since he'd arrived at her door yesterday. She was wearing her pale yellow sun dress, his favorite—it was warm enough for that—a garment which set off her dusky skin gorgeously. When they passed through a little village they stopped and picked up sodas, crackers-and-cheese packets, other junk food, and kept on driving. Angela fed him bites of the snacks and they shared a bottle of root beer. He felt like a kid, a teenager with his first girlfriend on their first outing alone together.

"I love you, you know," he said once, unable to contain himself.

She smiled enigmatically, moving her hand in his. "Okay."

In the afternoon they came to a ridge that overlooked a valley filled with miles and miles of breathtakingly beautiful pine trees—what type exactly he didn't know—and they stopped to look at it for a while. White hawks circled lazily in the sky. Slowly they moved to each other to kiss, to make out in the car like adolescents, giggling and fumbling awkwardly with each other. The car windows were open and the fresh mountain air seemed to fill his soul, carry him to the most natural of highs.

She pulled away finally, grinning and whispering breathlessly, "We better stop."

He laughed. It was all right; nothing could detract from his happiness today. As they drove on he thought about school, about his classes, about Ron Hunter and his yoga and Meredith's mother Dora angry with him and the jamming copy machine and none of it mattered, all of it was lost, gone, in another world, a different, lesser world, not one to which he ever wanted to return. The wild natural world was all around him, multicolored, brilliantly alive. A stunningly attractive woman he loved was next to him, her little hand in his. He was free, he thought, now, here, free forever.

◙◙◙

When the very nice lady proprietor of the B & B left them alone in their elaborately Victorian second-floor suite, they made a cursory inspection of the handsome, frilly bedroom and bathroom and the lovely little private balcony overlooking a velvety expanse of grass and oak trees. But when they stepped inside again and closed the door their hands were all over each other, pulling at their clothes, dropping back into the soft, deep bed. The late-afternoon light poured in on them through the lacy white curtains and Stillwater discovered that whatever problems he'd had the night before were gone now, triumphantly gone: entwined in each other they made love for hours, wildly, uncontrollably, as they never had before.

It was growing dark by the time they finally finished. Both of them were breathless, sweat-soaked, exhausted, yet after they were done it was almost as if they became shy with each other once more, as if they were amazed at what they'd just done and couldn't quite explain it to themselves. They lay side-by-side, not touching except for their fingertips.

"Good Lord," Angela said, staring up at the ceiling, a little giggle in her voice. "What the hell was all *that?*"

"I don't know."

"It's like—like the last time you make love before the end of the world."

He laughed. "Yeah."

They dozed as the room grew darker.

"We need to have dinner," she said.

"Do you want to go out?"

Turning, she snuggled against him. "Not really."

"Do we still have any of those cheese-and-crackers things?"

"Yeah. Cookies, too. And root beer. It's warm now, though."

"Sounds like the greatest dinner of all time."

"It does!"

They ate and drank naked on the bed like shameless children, like Adam and Eve before the fall. Everything was delicious, insanely so. The dinner was a hilarious gigglefest of empty wrappers tossed on the floor, spilled root beer, crumbs licked off each other's chins.

"I do love you," he said, when the dinner was done and the room was all but black. They were sitting cross-legged, facing each other. He could see only her silhouette outlined against the white lace curtain.

"I love you too, Terry," she murmured, leaning her face to him, pushing her lips onto his chest. "I do."

"Will you marry me?"

"Yes."

They hugged gently. He kissed her hair again and again and then separated again, sitting contentedly together.

"I need a shower," she said finally.

"So do I. Is it big enough for two?"

"Not really. It's a little one. Do you mind if I go?"

"No. I'll take one right after. Then we can pick up where we left off."

She laughed. "Amigo," she said, touching his cheek, "I love you, but I'm *done!*"

This sent both of them into gales of hilarity. She stood up then, walked in the darkness to the bathroom, flipped on the light. "Jesus, my legs are shaking!" she called to him. Stillwater sat back happily, chuckling. He heard her using the toilet. Then the shower turned on and he heard the curtain being pulled back and then forward again and the sound of the water flow breaking up as she stood under it.

His phone rang.

He flinched; he'd forgotten he even had his phone with him. It was in the pocket of his jeans, which were collapsed on the floor next to the bed.

He stared at the slight bulge where he knew the phone was. The jeans were dim in the reflected light from the bathroom. The phone *bleeped* again and again. Then it stopped. He sat there unmoving, his pulse quickening.

After a minute or two the phone began bleeping again.

He recoiled this time, pushed his back up against the headboard, covered his legs with the bed sheets. Stop it, he tried to instruct the device through his mind. Stop it.

It stopped.

No doubt it was nothing. Most of the calls he got at this time of night were telemarketers. It certainly wasn't the school; he'd called first thing that morning, telling them he was sick and explaining where his substitute packet was. No one from the school would be calling him, not at this hour. It could even be that damned yoga center, reconfirming his appointment or trying to get him to sign up for costly new classes. He couldn't think of anything else it might be. Nothing. He might as well lean down and take the phone and flip up the cover and just look, just to satisfy his curiosity.

He did not pick up the phone.

Angela finished in the shower. The water stopped, the curtain was pulled back, and he heard the sound of a towel being efficiently whipped over her body. She stepped into the doorway, lit from behind by the bathroom light. Her head was cocked as she dried one of her ears with the towel.

"All yours," she said.

He sat looking at her, his heart flooded with feeling.

"Will you want kids?" he said.

She looked at him. "I don't know," she said. "I mean, you have two." She walked to the bed, leaned down onto it. "My biological clock is ticking. Would you want to?"

"I'd love to have kids with you. I love you."

She smiled, finished with the towel and tossed it playfully at him. "Take your shower, lover," she said, straightening again and starting to pick up the mess of wrappers and clothes on the floor.

He stood, smiling, and made his way to the bathroom, tossing her damp towel in the corner by the sink. He started the water and stepped in.

"Terry?" she called.

"Yes?"

"Your phone is ringing."

He felt himself breathing. "Just leave it," he called back. "I'll check it later."

He should have smashed it, he realized too late. As he was standing up it would have been a simple thing to accidentally step on it. It was hidden in his jeans, his jeans were on the floor, it would have been the most natural thing in the world. One step. Broken. Useless. No longer a part of him, of them, of the two of them together in their new life. But he hadn't thought of it.

He stood in the shower a long time.

"Terry?"

"Yes."

"It's ringing again."

"Just—turn it off, Angela. Or—no, I'll come out." He switched off the water, toweled himself dry quickly.

"It's there on the floor," she said. "I think it's in your pants pocket."

"Never mind that," he said. "Come here."

She smiled, stepped into his arms. "I told you, amigo, I'm done. I'm tired!"

"What time is it?"

"I don't know. Pretty early. But it's been a long day."

"It has."

She stepped back. He was shocked at how beautiful she was, standing naked in the dim light. "Don't you want to check your phone?"

"Tomorrow."

"It could be important, Terry. What if it's Jodie? Or Nelson?"

"It's not Jodie. It's not Nelson. I—please, Angela, I don't even want to think about it now. Here. With you. There's plenty of time to think about all that when we get back. We'll have the rest of our lives together to deal with things. Now I—I just want to be with you. Tonight."

She smiled. "Well, you do have a way with words, mister, I'll say that." She looked through the laced curtain of the window. "You know, I think it's starting to rain."

"Wow. Good timing. I mean, that we're here and together and all cozy like this."

She smiled at him. "Definitely."

They got into the bed, pulling just a light sheet over themselves, and held each other. For a while they faced one another, then she turned away and he spooned the full length of her body as she stroked his forearms. After a time he drifted into a shallow sleep, still aware of his surroundings but finding the darkness populated now with images of her standing in the doorway drying her ear with the towel, of their awe at the beauty of the blazing West Virginia sugar maples, of the ravenous dinner the night before, of writing *Gone to soccer game at school* on a Post-It Note and affixing it to the handle of the refrigerator, of fleeing the store with the ice cream, of apologizing to Meredith Bennington, of the copy machine jamming with his Hemingway quizzes, of the Absurd Man, of Ron Hunter selling him on the value of taking up yoga, of getting into the shower that morning and noticing spatters of blood on the tops of his feet, *Don't worry, Terry, I'm fine, it washes right out.*

The phone bleeped and he jerked instantly to consciousness again.

"Terry," she said sleepily, "answer your phone."

"No, it's—it's all right." His breathing was shallow, rapid.

"Well, answer it or shut it off. But I think you should answer it."

He listened to it bleep.

She pushed him slightly with her elbow. "I mean it, Terry. Pick it up."

He threw the sheet back and fumbled in the dark for his pants. As he did so, the phone stopped bleeping again.

Extracting it from his pocket, he flipped up the top and, not looking at the screen, muted the device. Then he put it back in his pocket and tossed the jeans on a chair.

"Important?" she asked from the bed.

"Telemarketer."

"Oh. Well, you turned it off, right?"

"I turned it off."

"Okay. Come back to bed."

He did, though this time his mind would not loosen and drift. He was somehow convinced that the phone was going to ring again. He knew it was turned off, that a million people could call his number and leave a million messages and he would never hear one of them, not a single one. Yet somehow he didn't believe it. He wondered if he could get up and go to the bathroom, accidentally step on the goddamn thing, but no, he'd placed it in the chair, it was no longer on the floor. Maybe once she was asleep he could get up and wrap the phone in a towel and press down slowly with all his force and break it silently so that she wouldn't know, break it and then put the pieces on the floor and later get up and pretend that...

He watched himself from a high place. He watched as the thin, gaunt man with his arms around the lovely nude woman stared into the blackness, eyes wide, bewildered. He watched as the gaunt man started to gasp, his breath coming short. He watched as the man's Adam's apple began to bob up and down. He watched as his hands began to shake.

Angela's breathing had become deep and steady. He extricated himself from her slowly, carefully, and sat up, moving his legs over the side of the bed. It was raining steadily now; he could hear it spattering the window. He walked over and looked out, brushing the lace curtain aside and staring at the black sky and the glistening street below.

Then he turned and walked to the side door that led to the little balcony. He opened it as quietly as he could and stood staring into the darkness. The air had turned cold and goose bumps covered his naked body. As he gazed at the rain it seemed to him that each descending drop streaked the sky like a falling star. They were bright that way, supernaturally intense. He stepped out into the rain, stood there in the night with the stars that were raindrops cascading down onto him.

Behind him he heard the phone bleeping.

But it was not his phone; the ringtone was different. It was hers. He heard her moving in the bed, rustling in her bag which was hung on the bedpost. As she rummaged around she called, "Terry, what are you doing? Close the door, it's cold!"

He stood unmoving as the sky dropped down on him, the melting stars of the sky that would wash away blood and tears and emptiness and loss and death.

He could hear her voice inside the rain but not the words, just the tone. It started sleepily indifferent and then became sharper, more focused, and finally grew concerned, confused, frightened.

"Terry?" she called.

He did not answer. He raised his head and let the rain of stars pelt him, flood him, smash him to redemption.

"*Terry?*" she called again.

He stood unmoving, at one with the cold sky and the enfolding night.

Then her voice was directly behind him, unavoidable.

"Terry? Honey?"

He turned at last and looked at her for the last time, the last time like this.

She was holding the phone toward him in her outstretched hand, her face a mask of perplexity and fear.

"Terry," she said softly, "you have to take it. It's for you."

Skating the Shattered Glass Sea

◯◯◯

When the gate opened—when the blandly expressionless nurse pulled it slowly back and it creaked, yes, it *did* creak very slightly as he walked through—what Timothy Wake felt was neither fear nor foreboding, either of which he might have expected. What he felt was anguish.

It hit suddenly and entirely without warning, a sickening sensation of dropping, falling somehow inside himself, his stomach lurching and a certainty of doom overwhelming his senses. He was aware of the nurse—"Frobisher," her name tag read, her face all steep planes and angles like an El Greco martyr—shutting the gate behind him. He stopped in the middle of the hallway, nearly doubled over.

"Are you all right, sir?" she said, briskly efficient, moving to him.

It began to pass off a little and he managed to stand more or less straight again. "Yes—just a cramp. I'm fine."

She studied him carefully. He knew what she was thinking: Was this old man in his too-formal suit about to collapse? Should she have him sit down, take his blood pressure, check his pulse?

"Really," he said, trying his best smile of reassurance. "I'm all right." His voice was thin, emotion tightening his throat. He loosened his tie slightly.

But now her look changed. She cocked her head curiously. "I'm sorry," she said, "but you look familiar to me. Have we met?"

"Ah." He got this often. "You may have seen me on TV."

"Oh, yes. You're a...a news broadcaster, is that right?"

"An actor."

"Oh, of course." She nodded. "But I can't quite..."

He named a few of the better-known programs he'd been in, mostly one-shot guest appearances, mostly years ago.

"Yes, I'm sure I've seen you in some of those," she said, smiling vaguely. "Welcome to Golden Canyon Behavioral Health Center, Mr. Wake." She resumed leading him up the hall. He imagined she had no real memory of anything she'd seen him in. He had that kind of face. He had that kind of career.

It wasn't until they arrived at the door of room B10 that it occurred to him there might very well be another reason she found him so oddly familiar. After all, behind the door resided his twin sister.

She'd been there for more than fifty years. Well, perhaps not behind this particular door, no—but this building, this institution, this asylum. This warehouse of the mad which Tim had never once in his life visited. Until today.

The anguish seemed to permeate his being, causing his skin to tingle and his heart to race. He wished desperately that this professionally pleasant nurse would not open the door, would say to him *I'm sorry, there's been a mistake, your sister isn't here, she's been transferred to another building in another county, another state, another country.* And he would run wildly away, shoving the gate aside or crashing through it and charging out into the parking lot, leaping into his car and pulling out and never, never coming back.

But no: the nurse was knocking softly at the door now. "Miss Wake? Miss Wake, you have a visitor."

There was no response. The nurse opened the door.

The room was small and dark; a single lamp glowed on a little table. There was a narrow bed, neatly made. An old woman wearing a plain blue house dress and white socks sat on the floor, her back against the bed. Her hands moved gently and slowly in the air, up and down, making invisible patterns to no apparent purpose. She did not look up as the nurse entered the room.

"Miss Wake?"

Tim looked at the aged creature on the floor making her designs in the air and opened his mouth to say *There's been a mistake, that's not my sister.* But he said nothing, realizing that of course he inevitably pictured Lily in his mind as a twelve-year-old girl; he still carried a picture of her from that time in his wallet. She'd stopped aging the day she was hospitalized all those years ago—stopped, that is, in his mind. Not in reality.

In reality her hair was thin, wispy, ghost-white; deep crevices lined her face. Her lips were badly chapped, cracked and flaking. She seemed to possess virtually no muscle anywhere; her skin appeared to hang directly over her bones like a loose sack. Her ever-moving hands were roped with ugly blue veins. She seemed smaller than he remembered, as if the years had diminished her; he supposed that they had. They had certainly diminished him.

"Miss Wake, your brother is here to see you. Your brother, Miss Wake."

At that the woman looked up. Her eyes, once a brilliant and piercing blue, were washed out now, to the point that they really had no color at all. There were dark pockets under them. Her eyebrows, what little was left of them, were the same pale, lifeless color as her skin.

The nurse smiled. "She'll be fine," she said reassuringly to him. "Miss Wake is one of our most tranquil patients. She's very quiet and peaceful. She rarely speaks."

"What—" it was almost impossible for him to speak—"what does she...do? Here?"

"Do? Oh, we have many programs here, as I know they told you out front. Miss Wake likes finger painting—we have several of her pieces hanging in the common rooms, you should take a look before you go. She's really very talented. And she likes television. Perhaps she's seen you there from time to time."

He did not respond.

"I'll leave you two alone," she said at last. "We ask that you please leave the door open. I'll be by from time to time to look in. Please don't hesitate to tell any member of the staff if you need anything."

With that she smiled her professional smile and stepped out of the room. He heard her footsteps fading down the corridor. He was surprised at how quiet the place was; he'd imagined screaming madwomen being pulled through the hallways in straitjackets. Yet this was just like any well-run, quiet hospital. The fixtures were old, certainly, the hallways dim; but everything seemed clean and orderly.

He looked at the old woman for a long time. Finally he knelt down to her.

"Hello, Lily," he said at last.

She didn't respond, didn't acknowledge his presence in any way. He watched as her hands moved in the air. The movement wasn't rushed or frantic; rather it was slow, considered, even graceful in a way. She seemed extremely intent on whatever it was she thought she was doing. Oddly, for some reason he found himself thinking of palaces: great shining glass palaces with elaborate towers and turrets, shining windows and parapets. What a strange thing to occur to him, he thought, here, in this place.

He watched her for a long moment, puzzled, and then felt pain beginning in his knees. He stood and moved to the single chair in the room, pulled it away from the desk and turned it to her. He sat down on it and studied her for a while.

"Lily? It's Tim. It's Tim, Lily."

He thought she glanced at him, but it was hard to say; her eyes generally followed the motions of her hands. As he looked at her eyes he recognized—yes—that hers were something like his. His own were much clearer, they lacked the indescribable vagueness that hers possessed; but the color, that washed-out light blue, like tinted glass left fading for years in the sun, was the same.

No one would have realized that they were twins. She'd become bony and frail, while he was heavyset now, almost beefy, and the work he'd had done on his face and hair (a little, *not* a lot) made him look younger than he was. He knew he could pass for sixty. She looked closer to eighty.

He reached into his breast pocket and brought out his wallet, touched the old photo he knew was there. He'd looked at it a hundred times in the past week, since deciding to make the drive from Los Angeles to Arizona to see Lily one more time before the end, the end he was now quite sure was coming, and soon: grim-faced Dr. Clayton had told him so at Cedars-Sinai, gently but in no uncertain terms, as she looked at the x-rays and test results. The cancer had returned— returned and metastasized, running riot now through his veins and nerves and muscles and bones. They'd discussed his options, none of which were promising. Six months. A year.

And so he'd made the drive while he still could, while he still felt well enough to do it. In a few months he wouldn't be able to, he knew. Yet he'd always known he'd make the drive someday. He'd put it off for decades, but he'd always known that Lily was here, poor dear mad lost Lily, in this hospital in

Arizona. He paid for it, after all, though he never saw any bills; his accountant took care of everything. Every year, year in and year out, for more than half a century. After Mother and Father had died in the car crash, the estate had paid for her care—God knows there had been plenty of money—and then once his career was established he'd taken it over himself. And this is what he'd been paying for, he now saw. This dim room, this feeble lamp, this old woman with her hands moving aimlessly through the air.

"Lily? Look."

He held the photo where she could see. Her hands slowed for a moment and, yes, she definitely looked at the photo. It was her, it was the two of them together, black and white, when they were about twelve: not long before the end. They stood grinning in bathing suits, eyes squinting in the bright sun, bare arms unselfconsciously touching. It must have been around 1960, he thought, surely summer: it would never have been warm enough to be dressed like that at any other time on the Oregon coast. He imagined their mother must have taken the photo, but wasn't sure; they looked too relaxed for either of their parents to have been present. Possibly it had been one of their many guests, the bohemians who occupied the big house during the season. He could imagine Lily running to one of the painters or poets wandering around on the beach and calling eagerly, *Sir, would you take our picture? Please?*

It was not obvious that the children in the photo were twins, but they were clearly siblings—the same smiles, cheekbones, noses, eyes, eyebrows. Lily was cute in the old image, her grin toothy, short dark hair pushed back behind her ears, body still that of a little girl except for the hint of new breasts under the swimsuit. As for himself, he looked to his own eyes like any twelve-year-old boy in a pair of swimming trunks. Shirtless, scrawny. He felt no connection to that boy at all.

"Remember, Lily?" he said, his voice shaking slightly. He cleared his throat. "Remember this? That's you." He pointed. "And that's—that's me. A long time ago."

Her hands did not stop moving in the air but she looked, she *did* look.

"Do you remember, Lily?"

Her eyes wandered from the photograph back to the invisible space before her. He thought for a moment she'd said something, but then realized that it was just the sound of her breathing, a light whistle and wheeze.

Impossible to imagine, now: that these two people, himself and this woman, had once been the same. From the same womb, growing up in the same place at the same time, spending nearly all their time together. His twin. There had been a time that the idea had seemed as natural as air. Of course he had a twin, *his* twin, his sister Lily. Everyone knew that. Everyone knew they lived in the big rustic house on the Oregon coast where all the artists came—they called it "The Cabin"—where Mr. and Mrs. Wake sponsored their colony of creative types in between long bouts of martinis and cigarettes and affected sophistication. Neither of their parents were artists themselves, but with their mother's family wealth they were able to collect artists like seashells. All types—sculptors, writers, dancers, musicians who in the evenings would serenade the crowd at the piano in the sitting room or strum their guitars on the patio facing the rocky beach. These people never brought children, and so he and Lily would have the place to themselves as Mother and Father would be far too preoccupied with their guests (some of them quite celebrated—Robert Lowell, George Balanchine, Jackson Pollock, Carson McCullers; even Leonard Bernstein once or twice). The days were quiet and orderly for the most part, people working on their projects diligently in their rooms, the two house servants taking care of everything; but evenings after the servants departed would be boozy and smoky, the house crowded with chaotic people. As often as not their parents would forget to provide them any dinner, or Mother would pour some canned spaghetti into a pan and leave it on the stove, neglecting it until it was scorched black. He and Lily would raid the kitchen then, happily stuff Oreo cookies and Ritz crackers and Coke into themselves.

For as packed a house as it often was, Tim remembered, the two of them were quite often alone. They spent hours together in one or the other's bedroom, drawing, reading, listening to records, making up little plays for their puppet theater, watching TV on a little set with a perpetually wavy black and white picture. The sounds of the nightly party downstairs rarely let up until two or three in the morning and they wouldn't bother to try to sleep until then. They rarely talked much; there was no need for talk between them. They *knew* each other. They were, he'd thought, not two separate people, not really, but two parts of the same person. When one was hungry, the other was hungry. When one was restless, the other was restless. And when they did talk—when they had to—they finished each other's sentences as easily and naturally as if they spoke in a single voice.

None of this had seemed strange to Tim then. It was all he'd ever known; anyway, everyone knew that twins invariably shared connections other people didn't. Their parents and teachers found it "cute," nothing more.

They would run together on the beach in the moonlight, the sound and light of the house far behind them. He could remember the sound of her fast breathing in front of him, her light giggle as he chased her. Huge heavy sea-rocks blocked most access to the water itself. Their parents' beach was not really a place for bathing in the surf; anyway, for most of the year it was cold, mist-gray and often raining. But when the weather turned warm they investigated, night after night, while the adults drank and smoked and laughed back at the house. They discovered that there were pathways through the rocks, narrow passages where there were no jagged stones underfoot, where you could pass directly out into the crashing salt water. They soon memorized those paths and so were able to splash around, shrieking with delight, in the darkness. As far as Tim could remember, no one ever noticed they were missing; their parents never asked where they'd been. There was a back door he and Lily would use to come back in.

The old memories spattered him now like sea spray. He'd buried this part of his life half a century ago. Yet with this unfamiliar old woman before him, they came alive again: things he'd not thought of in decades, ever since Mother and Father died and he had hitchhiked down to Los Angeles, all of sixteen years old, determined to be an actor. His life had been simple then, sleeping on Venice Beach, going to auditions. He pretended to be a poverty-stricken young artist like everyone else there; of course he wasn't. Mother and Father had left an estate worth over two million dollars, of which he received a fairly generous monthly allowance until his twenty-first birthday, when he came into it all. His parents' contacts in the film industry served him well; he fairly quickly found himself in small roles in soap operas and minor TV dramas. He attended Actors Studio West, honed his craft, found himself disliking Hollywood types and, more attuned to live theater anyway, began his long years doing everything from Shakespeare in Ashland, Oregon to Tennessee Williams Off-Broadway to *The Pajama Game* in, quite literally, Hoboken, New Jersey. An occasional small role in TV or film. A couple of marriages—thankfully, no children—along with countless liaisons. All the time skating over the shattered remnants of what had once been his life at The Cabin with Lily, with Mother and Father, never revisiting any of it even for a moment. It was the only way, the only way that wouldn't be so painful as to destroy him. Staying focused. Staying free. It was how he lived. How he *had* to live.

And his sister? His sister was in the Golden Canyon Behavioral Health Center in Arizona. Then. Now. Forever.

The best such place in the western part of the country, so his parents had been told after months of therapies had failed with her. Just after she turned thirteen, she'd been committed. Mother and Father moved there for a while, to the little town nearby, to be close to her; Tim stayed at The Cabin, kept going to school. A year later came the traffic accident, Father drunk at the wheel: head-on into the cab of a tractor-trailer. Miraculously, the truck's driver suffered only minor injuries. Mother and Father were smashed to jelly.

He tried to say some of this to Lily now, to this old woman with her arms swaying in the air, but could manage only a few words. The anguish squeezed his heart, made his breath come short and shallow.

"Lily? Lily, I..."

Her hands, why did she not stop moving her hands? What was she doing? Surely there was medication to control this condition, surely she should have some sort of treatment, what had he been paying for all these years?

"I—I brought you something else," he said at last, putting the photo down on the bed. He suddenly realized that he was trembling and forced himself to breathe, breathe deeply, breathe slowly. "I brought you something else, Lily."

He reached into his pocket again and brought out a small sack, poured its meager contents into his palm.

"Remember these, Lily?"

Her hands slowed and she looked.

"Sea glass," he said, picking up one of the small colored objects. This one was an opaque pale blue, as perfectly shaped as a smooth stone. "See, Lily?"

His heart jumped as, for the first time, her hands stopped moving in the air. She turned her full attention to him, gazing closely at the little glass stones in his palm. She reached to touch one, then pulled back suddenly, looking at him.

"It's all right," he said gently. "It's all right, Lily. They're for you. I brought them for you. Sea glass."

As children they had haunted the beach in search of them, these bits of broken glass softened and smoothed and polished by the sea. They would hold pieces of it up to the light, watch the sun's rays shine blue and green and pink through onto the sands, onto themselves. They would dream of where it had come from, off a pirate ship perhaps, a bottle of rum—Yo! Ho! Ho!—dropped into the ocean hundreds of years ago, broken up on the bottom, dashed against rock and coral, then slowly tumbled and rolled toward their shore, massaged by the waves and sand for centuries until the bits emerged from their sea-chrysalis like tiny glass butterflies for them to touch, to hold and share. They'd collected such specimens: dozens of examples in wicker baskets sat in both their rooms.

Carefully, she moved to him again, picked up the clear blue piece, held it close to her eye.

"It's beautiful, Lily, isn't it?"

He watched her. He'd gone back to Oregon just before he'd made the drive here, not back home—The Cabin was no longer there, anyway, having been replaced years ago by condominiums—but to a similar beach a few miles from it. There he'd wandered for an hour or two, searching. He'd found a few examples, washed them carefully, put them in the little sack for her.

She took the other sea-stones then, picking up each from his palm one by one. She hunched over them, studying them intently.

"They're for you, Lily. For you."

She looked at him, her expression quizzical. Then she smiled suddenly. Her teeth were unfamiliar; he realized suddenly that she wore dentures. Her attention returned then to the sea glass. She held the pieces cupped in her palms, close to her face. Suddenly she turned to the bed, grabbed the photograph, held it together with the little stones. Her body began to rock gently: forward, back, forward, back. She made a quiet moaning sound.

"Lily?" he said quietly. "Are you all right, Lily?"

She pushed the items into her right hand and with her left she reached out to him, took his fingers and looked at him. She pulled lightly at his hand. Imagining that he understood, he slipped down out of the chair to sit facing her on the floor. She stared at him for a long time, her expression unreadable. He found himself looking at the stones, at the open doorway, at anything but her. Strange. On stage he could stand listening to an actor's monologue for many minutes at a time, holding eye contact, unmoving, and feel not the slightest bit self-conscious about it. But he could look at his sister's eyes only briefly.

Finally she put the stones and the photo on the floor between them and took both his hands tightly and stared at them.

It was then that he remembered, that it came rushing back like a massive wave at high tide. It hit him like that, with a nearly physical force: he all but fell backwards at the impact.

The palaces. The palaces that he and Lily had made together, made for each other. Like something out of *The Arabian Nights:* glass, or what looked like glass, enormous elaborate structures that they would build together in her room or his, high opaque walls, spiraling towers, smooth bright gates and bejeweled doors and golden staircases and graceful bridges and spires, all impossibly fragile, impossibly beautiful, and theirs, only theirs, theirs alone, where they could live free of that other world, the world of parents and other people and other places. Here was where they belonged. They both knew it. They didn't have to say it.

What were the palaces made of?

He couldn't answer that. They just *were.* Hour after hour they would build them, changing details, redesigning, alone in their own personal world, the only world that ever mattered. They loved them, loved constructing them, loved making them together. The palaces were not bound by any rules of the world: they were magnificent in their impossibility, their utter lack of plain quotidian utility. They were the most beautiful things Tim had ever seen, and Lily too, yet if Mother or Father happened to wander in, the palace would simply vanish. It would no longer exist.

How did they build them?

He didn't know. He'd stopped thinking about it half a century ago, ceased remembering it, buried it. They were made of nothing, he tried to tell himself. They were nothing. Children's fantasies, that's all they'd been. And yet they would work for hours not on separate palaces, but on the *same* palace: moving their hands, a gate would expand or shrink, a turret would change color, a wall would shift. They wouldn't talk. They would just build happily, content in their work as only children can be. Even then, it wasn't something he thought about; it was just the way he and Lily were. They would live together, he'd thought then, *be* together always, building palaces, running on the beach. They needed no one else. They were one organism, a single self. It never even crossed his mind that anything would ever be different.

He looked at her.

At last he tore his hands from hers, stood clumsily, turned away, staring stupidly at the desk and the lamp.

He'd known for fifty years that it had not been his fault, that it was the fault of their martini-drenched parents for leaving them so constantly unsupervised, in such a sloppy, incoherent atmosphere. What did he and Lily know of danger? When they were together, nothing seemed dangerous. Climbing on the craggy wet rocks by the light of the moon did not seem dangerous. They were kids together, they loved each other, they were one person. He'd been scampering about on the rocks, watching how the water glowed in the blue-lit dark. He hadn't known. For minutes he hadn't. And then he did: Lily, face-down in the water. Even then he'd thought it a joke, the kind they often played on each other, so for a moment he'd just laughed. But when she didn't move a sickening hard thing seemed to slice through him and he leapt down into the dark water crying her name and pulling her up and onto the beach. Her head lolled. There was a terrible wound on her left temple, she wasn't breathing, he screamed *Lily! Lily!* and pressed his mouth to hers as he'd been taught to in First Aid training at school, he put his arms together and pressed down on her chest again and again, more breathing, and at last she coughed and choked and turned suddenly onto her side and vomited and then everything was all right again.

But it wasn't. Despite the adults rushing onto the beach, it wasn't. It wasn't when they helped her into the house, when Mother cleaned the wound on her head—she'd slipped on the wet rock—and wrapped it with a bandage, when his father called an ambulance and an ambulance came, it wasn't. It had seemed to be for a little while. But it wasn't.

Lily was never the same again. She became vague, disorganized, easily confused. Sometimes she was almost as she'd been, but many others she seemed uncertain where she was, unclear who exactly was around her. Even him, her twin, her other self.

She was pulled out of school. She stayed home.

They were no longer one person. Lily was hardly a *person* at all, now. This girl looked like Lily but she wasn't, not really. Her movements were awkward and tentative in a way they'd never been before. When she talked her words came out more slowly. Her eyes took on a permanently vague expression, as if they were clouded over by something no one else could see.

Her eyes, Tim knew with horrible clarity, were the same now, more than half a century later. They were washed-out, they looked weary and old, but the expression had not changed. Why had he come here? he wondered.

He no longer knew.

He wiped his eyes with his hand and breathed. The anguish sat heavy and awful in the pit of his stomach. He knew he would never return to the Golden Canyon Behavioral Health Center. He would never return to the Arizona desert. He would go home, insofar as Los Angeles was his home, and soon enough he would die. Curtain. The end.

He sighed deeply, feeling lost and futile. At last he turned around to face his sister: the photo and sea-stones sat before her, but she was not looking at them. Her arms were moving in the air again.

He knew he could not stay any longer—that if he did he would crumble, break, fly apart.

He stepped close to her, leaning down and kissing her on the top of her head.

"Goodbye, Lily," he said, keeping his voice as steady as he could manage.

He stepped to the doorway, his vision dark. He stumbled into the hall.

"Tim?"

He stopped. It was an unfamiliar voice—rough, husky, an old woman's voice.

The voice had come from her room.

"Tim, Tim, *Tim!*"

Alarmed, frightened, he turned and stepped into the doorway again.

His sister was sitting there on the floor, her hands in the air. But she was looking toward him, her eyes clearer than before, her expression one of unbridled joy.

In front of Lily was a palace. It was sky-blue and green and pink, seemingly made of glass but no, not glass, something infinitely more delicate and fragile. The walls and turrets were three or four feet tall and the entire structure glowed as if from within. As her hands moved in the air more depth and detail was added to the structure.

Yet things were badly wrong with this palace. The huge dormer windows all seemed to have been blown out, leaving jagged bits like crystal teeth in the frames. The tall spires were broken off at the top, the rubble remnants fallen on the floor. The walls were wildly uneven, jutting out at weird angles, disjointed, crooked, collapsing. The colors everywhere were dark, malevolent, sickening. All the proportions were wrong, disturbingly wrong, a palace seen in a fun house mirror, not one in which anyone could live, or would ever want to. It was a horrific structure, a palace out of a nightmare.

The sight repelled him.

He fell against the wall, his knees buckling. Behind him, from the doorway, came a voice: Nurse Frobisher's. He looked at her.

"What in the *world*...?" Her expression was utterly astonished. "Miss Wake," she said, "what...?"

Tim looked toward his sister again.

The palace was gone.

Nurse Frobisher stepped carefully into the room. "Mr. Wake, I'm sorry, I...I thought I saw...the most astounding thing...it was..."

He stood upright again, forced himself to control his breathing. Lily's expression had returned to what it had been before. Her hands moved again in the air, the empty air.

"There was nothing, Nurse Frobisher," he said in a voice as firm and authoritative as if he were reciting Shakespeare. "Nothing...Just Lily and I. And the souvenirs I brought her. You see?"

She stared at the photo and the sea glass that sat before Lily. "Yes," she said. "I see." She looked at him again. "It must have been..."

"A trick of the light."

"Of course."

He breathed: slowly, slowly. "I'll be going now. Goodbye. Goodbye, Lily."

The nurse led him back through the hallway and the creaking gate. In the lobby she wished him a pleasant day. He smiled and thanked her. He was a professional actor, after all. He could do this. He made his way through the lobby and out the front door.

And he held it back. He held it back as he'd been doing for half a century. He held it back as he would continue to do for as long as he had left.

He held back his anguish, knowing that the moment he gave himself over to it, he would never again be able to stop it from shattering what remained of the ruined palaces of his life.

The Long Light of
Sunday Afternoon

◯◯◯

He would go out. He'd thought about it for much of the day, moving now and then to the front window to check the sky: tumorous silver clouds tumbling across, blotting the blue. Wind, a fair amount of it, but no rain. Yes, he could walk, perhaps to the old park at the bottom of the hill. It seemed safe enough. How long had it been since he'd gone to that park? How long, in fact, since he'd gone out at all?

He pondered it as he drank his late afternoon "tea," which was really just an infusion of various herbs he'd found growing on the property. He'd dried the leaves, chopped them extremely fine, and placed them in little mesh bags, which then went into an old metal tin for storage. The print on the tin read *Harney & Sons*, a tea-making company from many years before. He did still have tea—real tea, good black Earl Grey, in a different tin—but there wasn't much left and he rationed it carefully, only rarely making so much as a single cup. The tin was nearly empty. Once it was gone there would be, he knew, no more.

But going out, now: what of that? He sipped the weak but pleasant herbal brew and nibbled at the plain black bread, not too stale, he'd found in a cupboard for his dinner. Of course it was only just past the middle of the afternoon, far too early for what most people would have called dinner, but this would be his last food of the day. He ate little now. There was enough to eat—canned goods, baked things he made at home—but none of it interested him. He was rarely interested in anything these days, really. This worried him a bit, and made him determined to do things like go out, something he did less and less anymore. Sometimes he didn't leave the house for days on end. There seemed little reason to. He might step out onto his property with the dog for a few minutes, take a stroll around what used to be the lawn, but even that was hazardous now. Great chuckholes dotted the ground and huge ropy weeds, including what he recognized as some form of poison ivy, choked it. If he had a few nuts or bread scraps he would keep them in his pocket for the squirrels that were invariably about scrounging for food, moving in the strangely limping, uncoordinated way they all seemed to now. Perhaps they were rabid? Anyway, he would toss the food toward them, but made sure to keep his distance. Yet he was happy to help the squirrels as he could. It must, he thought, be very hard for them.

He finished the tea and bread, brushing the table clear of crumbs. (He didn't use plates if he didn't have to; they were too much trouble to clean.) He placed his cup in the sink and moved to the bedroom, pulled on his white sneakers, the ones with the good deep tread. He checked the pocket of his jeans to make sure he had his key, though there was little reason to lock the house now; he had nothing to steal, really. And yet as he thought it he knew he was wrong. He had food.

Stepping into the dim bathroom he picked up his brush and ran it through what remained of his hair. The brush was old and yellow and was missing many of its bristles, yet it was one of the only tangible items he had left from his childhood. His mother had run this very brush through his hair when she got him ready to go to kindergarten each day. Somehow the brush had never been lost, not in all these years, and one day a long time ago he'd found it in a dusty box in the attic. It had been with him at the beginning, he thought, and now it was with him at the end. He looked at himself in the mirror. What he saw did not shock him. A cadaverous old man, that's what he was. A pitiful few strands of hair on either side of his head. The eyes, once a vivid blue, now resembled the gray of used dishwater—though his vision was still good. The nose was red and its texture seemed pulpier than it had been, covered over with huge ugly pores. The lips, perpetually chapped, were thin and nearly invisible. He hadn't shaved in a few days and stubble salted his jawline. His ears had somehow grown bigger than they once were, or else the rest of him had shrunk; they seemed huge, like flappers at each side of his head, with hair sprouting from them. His shoulders seemed higher than they should be; he knew that was because he stood and walked with a hunch now, his spine permanently curved (at least he assumed it was permanent: he'd never seen an old man's spine magically straighten once it bent like this).

He was old, that's all. It didn't bother him; what he saw in the mirror was comfortably familiar. The only time it concerned him was when he happened to angle the medicine-cabinet mirror just so that it caught the reflection of the mirror on the bathroom door. At that point, in the double reflection, he saw not the usual reversed image that he knew but rather himself as he really was, as he would look to others, if there were any others. This was invariably disturbing, uncomfortably different—the lines like deep crevices, the dark splotches shockingly bright and ugly. He did his best never to look at himself that way.

He wondered what day it was. There was a calendar on the wall of the kitchen and, satisfied that he was as well put together as he could be, he walked there and looked. Each night before bed he carefully x-ed out the completed day and so was able to keep track. He never forgot, or he liked to believe that he didn't. To imagine that he no longer knew what day it was: that was truly horrifying. It was not a possibility he would consider. He looked at the calendar and found that today was Sunday, the third Sunday in February.

Winter, but one would hardly know it from the weather now. There had been nothing in the past three months that he would have thought of as winter. The cold had never been more than what he thought of as mid-autumn. There was no snow, ever. There hadn't been snow in years, in this place that used to get feet of it again and again during the winter months. That had changed, along with everything else.

At the closet near the front door he pulled his light coat from a hanger and put it on, buttoning it up the front. Then he placed his gray wool hat on his head. It wouldn't do to catch a chill; he had no medicine other than a small, half-empty bottle of old aspirin tablets. He pulled on his leather gloves and took up the wooden cane that had belonged to his grandfather, another item he'd found in the attic years before.

Granddad, he'd asked seventy years ago, looking up at the dashing, funny old man he'd loved, *why do you carry that cane?*

Why, to strike at ghosts, my boy, his grandfather had said, playfully jabbing at the air with it as if it were a sword. *If any come my way.*

"Here, boy. Come on now. Let's go."

The dog, a brown-and-white mongrel mix of spaniel and hound with enormous black eyes, long whiskery snout, and a perpetually grieved expression, appeared from the bedroom, moving as quickly as it could now. It was old too, and missing several teeth (just as he was himself). It smelled like an old dog, an odor a bit like damp carpet. A thin discharge leaked from its eyes all the time; the man would wipe it, but wiping didn't help much. The dog looked up at the man expectantly, expression mildly curious, tail wagging slowly.

"Let's go, now," the man said, and the dog perked up as it understood they were to walk together. It moved quickly to the door, tail swishing more rapidly. The dog loved to go out, but only if they were together. It had learned to be wary of solo jaunts.

The man opened the door cautiously, peering around the front porch and over what remained of the street. He wasn't really worried; he didn't truly expect to see anyone, but it was important to be careful. There was always the question of diseased animals. He'd seen strange wildcats roaming up and down this street several times. But everything seemed quiet now, so he stepped through the door, the dog following. The man closed the door and locked it. Replacing the key in his pocket, he moved carefully down the front steps, leaning on the cane, the dog snuffling ahead of him. He could remember when this front yard was actually a *yard*—many years ago, when he entertained here and guests would pull their cars (cars!) up the long sloping driveway. He could remember men asking him who took care of his grass, it was so luxurious and beautiful, and he could remember telling them. He could remember inviting such people into the house and handing them a cool glass of Chardonnay and making small talk. He could remember socializing on the rear deck, overlooking the similarly flawless back lawn, fireflies appearing and then vanishing in the air.

He moved onto the cracked and crumbling sidewalk, watching his steps carefully, while the dog zigzagged in front of him, sniffing everything in sight, occasionally stopping to lift its leg at a bush or tree. The man was very careful. It wouldn't do to take a sudden fall, to break a bone; he might never get back to the house, be stuck here as the long light of Sunday afternoon stretched and then faded and finally disappeared entirely, leaving him helpless in the dark of this violated world. Moving slowly, he looked up now and then at what remained of the neighborhood. The houses were dilapidated now, of course—dirty, gradually collapsing wrecks. It was easy enough to imagine what this street would look like in a hundred years: the houses falling to rubble, the street and sidewalk reclaimed by the most tenacious weeds and wild grasses. It would still be obvious that someone had lived here, at some time—but who, when?

The wind was strong, but not steady. Cold gusts, not unpleasant, lightly stung his face for a moment, then passed off again. The sound of the breeze in the elms and oaks that dotted the neighborhood was pleasing and he considered closing his eyes and just listening, but it would be a bad idea. Closing one's eyes was not a valid notion out here, not even for a few seconds. He had to remain alert. Still, the sounds were comfortingly familiar. The breeze, the tap of the cane with each step, the sound of his own sneakers slapping and crunching along the broken pavement. He'd often walked with his wife in shoes like these, shoes that had made the same sound.

His wife. His first wife, that is. Strange: he had been married twenty years, for the most part happily, to his second wife. They'd had a child together. But when he thought of "his wife" it was never her he thought of: it was his first, to whom he'd been married only four years, when they were both very young. There were no children from that union. Yet as his mind went back to earlier days it was as if the twenty-year marriage had hardly happened at all, vanishing faster than a firefly in the dusk. The four years of his younger days, though, lived on in his mind and imagination, even though it, and she, were a half-century dead.

At times he had trouble remembering anything specific about his second wife—he could manage to recall the color of her hair easily enough (auburn), but her eyes?—while the first, who had been so vague and ill-remembered for so long, was astoundingly vivid. They'd married too early, when both of them were still nearly children, and their life together resembled that of two irresponsible kids left to their own devices. A tiny apartment in a bad neighborhood. Arguments over nothing, jobs lost, bills unpaid. Screaming, a great deal of screaming. She had a habit of throwing things at him in her spoiled-child rages, her blonde hair swinging wildly, her feet kicking the baseboards. The relationship lurched on for a few years and then unceremoniously stopped when he moved out and filed for divorce. It was over, he'd thought; and it was. But now it came back to him in the way he remembered old men in his own youth saying that they could hardly remember what happened yesterday but that incidents from their childhoods were completely clear to them.

The second wife, on the other hand: that relationship had been solid from the beginning, sober, mature, responsible. Passionate, for a few years. They had loved each other. They had built a home. They had large extended social networks of friends and relatives. They were successful. It worked. For twenty years it worked, from his early thirties to his early fifties, when everyone who knew them considered them practically inseparable, one joined organism whose very names invariably rolled off people's tongues in virtually a single phonetic unit. They were the picture of a successful long-term couple. And now, try as he might, he couldn't recall any of it.

There were photos back home of him with the auburn-haired woman: their first Christmas together, house parties, cute moments kissing on the sofa or holding hands in the kitchen. He could look at such photos and feel as if they were of different people entirely, or at least that the man there was not him, that he had never been that man or even known him. But the few photos he had of the blonde girl threw him back to that life again, that young life.

"Hey. Come here." The dog was chewing on something the man couldn't see. After a moment it raised its head and trotted on again. It was a skinny thing, the dog. Yet he fed it well enough on old canned goods: soups, stews, tins of anchovies in tomato sauce.

But, he wondered, returning to his memories, did the photos really take him back to that old life? He stepped carefully over a raised crack in the sidewalk. He'd also noticed that, for all the vividness of his oldest memories, they weren't all true. He knew that. At night, in the darkness of his bedroom, the sound of unidentifiable whirring and clicking creatures outside the window, he would have sudden sexual images of the two of them together—wild, riotous images, thoroughly pornographic, that would have their basis in things they had done together but which were entirely more joyous and free than anything the two of them had ever really done. In truth, though he'd loved the blonde girl, they had been badly mismatched in bed. She'd tolerated his attentions, but never enjoyed them. She'd blamed him for it, and he was perhaps partially at fault: what had he known of pleasing a woman, at that age? She'd been his first. He hadn't known what he was doing, not really. He'd tried, but she'd been impatient and unresponsive. Yet in memory! In memory they were every great loving couple of history rolled into one, the distortions of time turning her into one of the most passionate partners any man could ever dream of.

She was dead now, of course. He didn't know it for a fact but the chances of her being alive were nil.

As he neared the bottom of the hill he thought he saw movement from the corner of his eye and he stopped suddenly, watched and listened, his grip tight on the cane. The dog was ahead of him, on the other side. Had something rustled beside that blue house? The wind rose, then dropped off again. He could detect nothing.

He kept on walking.

He could sense a good increase in his heart rate now; his body was responding to the walk, pumping blood efficiently through his veins. It felt fine. The longer he walked the better he seemed to feel. His vision was sharper, his sense of smell more acute. He increased his pace, and as he did the early memories began to fall away, as if he were literally leaving them behind, dropped onto the street. He felt more connected to the here and now, more aware of his surroundings. He wished he'd brought a snack for the dog.

The park rose before him. The elms and oaks were still in possession of about half their leaves and they waved to him in the wind like thousands of little multicolored hands. The grass was overgrown and wild, of course, to the point that people from years before might not have recognized this area as a park at all. But he remembered it as it had been. He remembered the children's things that had stood in the far corner: swing set, monkey bars. He'd played on them himself, once. Later he'd watched his son playing on them—carefully, studiously, as was his way. The boy had rarely smiled. He'd been small for his age, dark-featured, with a perpetually pensive expression on his face—as if he were all too aware of the trials to come and was none too happy at the prospect. He'd shown pleasure in other ways than smiling or laughing. He'd had a way of cocking his head just so and scowling that to others would have looked like anger but his father knew it was a sign of the boy's happiness. He saw it again and again when they were at the swings, or later, when the boy was licking an ice cream cone.

He was a strange boy, and it frustrated his father that he could not remember more about him. His son had vanished, like his auburn-haired mother, down a terrible sinkhole of forgetfulness. The boy existed now only in quick fragments: the swings, the ice cream cone, the pensive expression. He hadn't lived long.

Looking up, he saw something he hadn't known was here: at the entrance to the park was a small graveyard. The stones looked old, older even than he was, so it must have been here all along, it must have been here since he was a boy heading to the swings and the monkey bars with his grandfather close behind him. Yet he didn't remember it, not at all. He stopped and stared while the dog sniffed eagerly ahead of him. Stones green with age, pockmarked with time, sad stone angels guarding the souls of people long dead and utterly unremembered who surely required no protection. Yet there they were. There it was. A graveyard.

He stepped toward it, using the cane to carefully check the ground before him. Odd that the grass here was only a little overgrown, nothing a good lawnmower couldn't have taken care of. He felt the wind on his face as he looked down at first one stone then another, unfamiliar names, dates from ages ago, long before he was even born. How strange that he could have forgotten that this cemetery was here. How long had it been since he'd taken this walk? Was his mind slipping away from him at last? He was well aware of the possibility, of course, yet somehow he didn't feel frightened or disoriented. He knew where he was. He knew the route back to his house. There was nothing strange here except that he did not recall the old graveyard in which he now stood.

He noticed the dog, its tail brushing back and forth and its hind quarters wiggling, making its way up a small hill to a dark spot in the ground. Things seemed safe enough here, so he used the cane to help himself follow the dog.

"What's that, boy? What have you got?"

As he came up to the place where the dog had stopped, he saw that it was a freshly-dug grave, the rich earth of its sides smooth and black. Within the rectangular hole was a coffin made of what appeared to be highly polished mahogany. The coffin was open, and empty; its interior was lined with powder blue satin.

The old man looked around, but saw nothing unusual. The wind moved in the oaks and elms.

"What's this?" he asked quietly, almost whispering. The dog looked at him and then at the grave, clearly puzzled too.

He could feel the wind, strong now on his cheeks. He began to shiver. He leaned on the cane more heavily.

A sound caused him to turn suddenly. There, walking toward him with a stepladder in his arms, was his grandfather. The old man said nothing as he watched his grandfather place the stepladder inside the grave. Then his grandfather stepped away again and looked at his grandson. He gestured for him to use the stepladder.

But the old man did not move. He watched as the dog sniffed cautiously around his grandfather.

The afternoon was beginning to darken and the long light of Sunday afternoon cast its shadows behind the gravestones all around. It was then he noticed that his second wife was sitting on one of the gravestones looking at him. Her face held no expression. Her auburn hair was longer than he remembered, and he did not recognize the black dress she wore.

He walked slowly up to her, emotions churning within him. They looked at each other. Then from behind her stepped his son, small, dark-featured. The boy looked up at him, cocking his head. The look contained no anger, no reproach, no accusation. It contained no emotion at all.

He glanced down for a moment, adjusting the cane in his hand. When he looked up again he realized that on another gravestone nearby sat the blonde girl, his first wife, not pretty but impossibly young—as young as he'd been, once. Her dress was a simple pastel. Her face, like those of the others, held no discernible expression.

They said nothing but he could feel within his mind what they wanted him to do.

Carefully he stepped toward the grave and set his foot on the top step of the little ladder. It was solid enough, so he descended the several steps until he found himself standing awkwardly next to the coffin. There was really no room; he would quickly topple into the silk-lined box unless he decided to step into it voluntarily, under his own power.

He did so. Although it appeared comfortable enough from above, lying in the coffin was painful. A hard rod ran along the entire length of the thing, covered over by the satin, and it made his back hurt.

He looked up into what he could see of the world, now reduced to a rectangular box of light. They were there, all of them, looking down at him. His two wives. His son. His grandfather.

Slowly, the grandfather began to lift the stepladder out of the grave. The old man knew what he was supposed to do now. Fine, he thought. It was over now, anyway. Everything was over. He was exhausted. He could not continue.

He began to close his eyes and at that moment the dog peeked its head over the edge of the hole. He heard it whimper in consternation.

He looked at the dog for a long moment, its long muzzle and wiry whiskers, its black rheumy eyes gazing worriedly at him. Then he said, quite loudly, "Wait."

His grandfather took his hands away from the stepladder and watched him.

"No," the old man said at last. It was difficult to stand up from such an awkward bed and he struggled. "No." He righted himself, picked up the cane again and aimed it up at them as if it were a sword. He placed a foot on the bottom rung of the stepladder as his ghosts watched him.

"I thought I was ready," he said. "I'm not ready. I have too much to do. The dog—the dog must have his dinner, you see."

He climbed carefully out of the hole, watching his every step. By the time he was back up again, his dead relatives had vanished.

He touched the nose of the old mutt, who licked his hand appreciatively.

"Let's go home," he said.

When the two of them reached the edge of the graveyard, the man looked back and saw that the graveyard was gone. Now there were only the trees and wild grasses he'd always known.

"Not yet, huh, boy?" he said quietly. "Maybe tomorrow. But not today. Are you ready for your dinner?"

In the long light of Sunday afternoon, darkness swiftly approaching but not yet arrived, the old man and the dog made their way back home.

Grace

It was when she saw the closet—the closet she'd not seen or thought of in fifteen years, except in dreams—that Abby Winter truly knew she'd come home.

It had been easy getting here. The entire old block was being demolished to make way for a shopping complex, and there was construction equipment all around—trucks, bulldozers, other great angry-looking metal beasts whose names she didn't know. Huge piles of lumber and brick that had once been people's houses dotted the landscape. Wire fences surrounded everything and there were big-lettered signs warning *Construction Area* and *Keep Out* and *Men At Work*. But it was Sunday morning now, and there were no men at work.

The fence hadn't been difficult to breach. It was clearly designed more for intimidation than actual security; Abby had simply parked her car near an obvious space between two metal posts that were holding up part of it. The space was just wide enough to squeeze her body through. Walking past the big silent machines had given her an unsettled feeling, as if they might suddenly roar into life and chase her down, crush her, obliterate her. But she knew that the most fearful things of all were within the house itself, the house she hadn't seen in a decade and a half and which now rose defiantly before her, one of the only structures still intact in this old neighborhood, a silent sentinel waiting patiently for her return.

The actual house was unimposing. Abby was surprised at how small it was; just a simple one-story rancher, long and low and undistinguished. The paint she'd remembered as yellow seemed to have dirtied to an indifferent gray, or perhaps the later owners had repainted it; it didn't matter. It was the house, anyway. The house where she'd spent the first twelve years of her life, the house that for years she thought she would never bring herself to look upon again.

She wondered why she found herself thinking suddenly of horses. She'd never yet even seen a real horse when she lived here, though now she and David and the kids loved nothing more than to drive out to the stables and go riding on a sun-bright afternoon. But when she was a girl? No. She'd never even taken a pony ride then. How strange, this random jumble of thoughts. Horses, indeed. She shook her head in irritation.

Now she peered through one of the front windows of the house, saw dimly outlined in the shadows the general shape of a front room she remembered well. It too looked smaller than she'd expected.

You didn't do it, Abby, she could hear her mother insisting in her mind. *Understand? You didn't do it.*

Abby had never seen her frail, nervous mother again after that final, catastrophic night, the night when everything ended, the last night Abby had spoken a word aloud for nearly three years. All that silence, she thought. From ages twelve to nearly fifteen she hadn't uttered a sound—well, her foster parents would tell her later that she sometimes cried out in the night. But words?

No. No words.

Abby wondered momentarily what she would do if the door were locked to her old house—odd, she hadn't even considered the possibility until this moment. But it was open, as she discovered upon reaching forward and simply turning the knob. Why would anyone lock a house that was going to be demolished the next morning, anyway? She pushed the door in gently and moved slowly across the threshold.

Silence.

There was an unreality to it. Such a simple, nondescript little house, the same as the dozen or so around it, almost all of which were now piles of rubble outside. Yet *this* house— *this* house was the one that had driven her into years of wordlessness. The one that had landed her mother in the prison upstate, where she soon died broken and alone. *This* house.

But the house wasn't the important thing, of course. It was the man in it. "Daddy."

Not her father. Her mother never knew who Abby's father was, though of course she hadn't admitted this to her daughter; Mama claimed that her real daddy had died a war hero in Vietnam. But Abby had learned the truth eventually, when she'd ordered a copy of her birth certificate to be able to apply for a college loan. Under *Father*, big as life—or death—was the word "UNKNOWN."

In place of her father, then, in this house, had been Mr. Pike. Richard Pike. "Daddy."

Stepping through a narrow hallway she stood in the main room, which was hollow and empty. The carpet had been pulled up, exposing a raw, ugly floor, scratched and stained. A few nails rested atop a small stack of wooden planks in the corner. The windows were uncurtained, dirty and naked. Abby could hardly imagine a time that there had been life here. A big multi-patched leather sofa had once sat in the far corner with a battered coffee table in front of it; Mama's chair had been opposite it. The TV had squatted in the other corner, there. The carpet had been long green shag. She had walked across it, played on it. For a while, that is. When Daddy first arrived.

She remembered his hard, angular face, long and sallow, his depthless blue eyes, the buzzcut that she'd liked to touch at the beginning. She remembered how his cologne mixed with the smell of his cigarettes and the metallic odor of his many guns. She had liked the resulting aroma. For a while.

C'mere, big girl! she could hear him saying, putting aside a pistol or rifle he was cleaning. *Come to Daddy!*

Now she wandered into the kitchen, which was gutted. The refrigerator and stove were gone; the cabinet doors gaped open, the cabinets themselves empty of all but dust and dirt. Had she really stood here with Mama, watching her fry eggs for him, make waffles for him, get him his endless cans of beer? Yes, she had. For a while.

Yet none of it seemed real. None of those things had ever happened, not in this place. Not to *her*.

It didn't become real until she reached the closet. Then she knew, truly, finally, that she was home.

She stood staring at the door. It was just a plain wood-panel closet door. Tens of thousands of them must have been manufactured for houses just like this one.

For a long time she couldn't approach it.

The closet was inside what had once been her bedroom. But the room itself meant nothing to her; it was as empty and lifeless as the other rooms in the house. It was the closet which held her attention, which fixated her. The door. The closet door.

Who's been a bad girl? Who's been a bad little bitch?

I'm sorry, Daddy, I didn't mean it, I'm sorry!

His hand, as big as her head, grabbing her wrist, yanking her across the room. The panicked sensation that her arm would pop out of its socket, that he would tear her apart like a doll, throw pieces of her everywhere around the room. His massive palm swooping down once, twice, slapping her across the face and whipping her head this way and that until

her neck ached and her cheeks were numb and her ears rang
and he pulled open the closet door while she kicked and
screamed and tried to hold onto the doorframe.

Bitch! Get in there! Little fuckin' bitch!

The door would slam and she'd be thrown into darkness.
She'd hear the special latch which Daddy had installed slide
impenetrably shut.

And there she would stay.

At first he'd done it only when Mama wasn't home, before
he'd installed the latch. He'd shove her dresser in front of the
door to hold her there. Then after an hour or two he'd calm
down and she'd hear him pulling away the dresser again and
he'd open the door, looking in at her sheepishly.

*Lost my temper, big girl. You won't say anything about this
to your mama, will you? Hell, you know ol' Daddy don't mean
it. I'm all bark and no bite, you know that. Howzabout we drive
into town and get you some ice cream? We can see a movie,
too. Just let's keep this between us—okay, big girl? Okay, baby?*

She remembered watching him cleaning his gun
collection while he stared at sports on TV. At first he'd only
brought in a single hunting rifle, but later he had more—
handguns too, eight or ten of them. The rifles he kept
mounted on the wall; the handguns were in drawers
throughout the house. She would watch as he massaged oil
into them, peered down their barrels, cocked and uncocked
them.

*Don't you go touchin' any of these, now. They're dangerous.
They're Daddy's toys.*

She remembered wearing long sleeve shirts and scarves
to school even in hot weather to cover the bruises he'd given
her. Once he punched her right in the face, knocked her
unconscious—a gigantic purple blotch covered her right

cheek that no makeup could hide. She'd stayed out of school for a week. *Chicken pox,* Daddy said to the school officials on the phone. To Mama he said, *She walked into a door.*

And one night—Daddy was out drinking with his pals— she'd crawled up onto her mother's lap in her big chair and confessed in a whisper everything that was happening when Mama wasn't home. All of it. The punishments that involved her pulling down her pants, too, and Daddy poking and prodding her with his fingers until she bled.

Her mother had looked at her strangely. And in that moment Abby realized something that sent a trickle of ice water down her spine: *Mama already knew.*

Now she stood before the door of the closet. Cold sun poured through the windows. She noticed that the latch mechanism Daddy had installed was long gone; she could detect no trace of it.

She opened the door slowly.

Mama, why didn't you do anything?

For soon it was the closet all the time. She stopped going to school. She wasn't allowed any light or clothes. There was no bedding; she slept naked on the shag carpet. He made her put in a bucket for when she had to go to the bathroom. Each night, very late, he unlatched the door and she was told to go empty the bucket in the toilet and flush it. Then she would be given a tray of food and water by Mama, who would silently kiss her on the head. Abby would take the tray back to the closet. Her bucket, too. Then Daddy would slam the door and latch it. At first she'd screamed, but what Daddy would do to her then quickly made her stop.

The closet was where, for nearly a year, she lived her entire life. Until one night when, dizzy, weak, delirious, she'd tripped with her bucket of urine and had gone sprawling across the carpet of the hallway.

Stupid bitch! He'd kicked her in her stomach, forcing the air from her lungs. She couldn't scream, couldn't breathe. She could only look as he glowered down at her. He'd picked up one of his gray pistols. *Stupid bitch!*

Somehow she staggered to her feet. And somehow—she would never remember how—she fell against him, or threw herself at him. She remembered the odor of alcohol on his breath. They struggled. The pistol skittered to the carpet between them. She snatched it up and, clenching her eyes shut, pulled the trigger. The gun exploded like a cannon, bucking wildly in her hands.

When she opened her eyes again she saw what looked exactly like rain-covered rose petals spattered on the wall behind Daddy's head. He stared at her blankly, seemingly puzzled, as his body slid slowly down to the carpet, twitching and jerking. Finally he was still. That was all.

Then Mama was standing behind her, muttering, sighing, making odd little mewling sounds. She took the pistol gently from Abby's hands and looked at it.

You didn't do it, Abby, she said. *Understand? You didn't do it. I did it.*

Abby had nodded, and not spoken another word for nearly three years.

She looked into the closet now. It was about four feet deep, perhaps six feet long. The carpet, like the carpet everywhere in the house, had been pulled up to expose raw floor.

When she looked at the back wall of the closet, down low, near the baseboard, she was surprised to notice a crude, dimly visible shape—a little drawing of some kind. She had to lean close to make out what it was: a childish outline sketch of a horse, some six inches high.

In a blindingly vivid flash, she remembered. She'd done it during the long days, when the light from the space between the door and doorframe allowed a dim glow into the closet. She'd drawn it by scratching in the paint with her fingernail. The later owners had never repainted inside the closet, and she'd blanked it out of her memory for fifteen years.

Grace. That had been the name she'd given her little horse.

She'd drawn it in the day, refining it, giving it texture and detail, and at night she trained herself to dream of riding on Grace through warm green fields, across sunlit valleys and meadows. She'd never dared scratch any more artwork into the wall for fear of Daddy finding it and punishing her. Just Grace. Only Grace.

Now Abby dropped down into the closet again and slowly pulled the door shut. For a long moment it appeared to be pitch dark, but then as her eyes adjusted the familiar glow between the door and doorframe began. This, at least, was just as she recalled it.

I'm sorry, Abby, her mother had said, before they took her away. *But I love you. I've always loved you.*

Abby shut her eyes and her fingers moved slowly across the outline of the horse on the wall. It took only a moment: and she was with Grace again, riding in the sunshine as they had for countless hours when she was young. She felt the supple, muscular animal moving rhythmically beneath her legs like an extension of her own self. She breathed in the clean, cool air rushing past and smelled the green living things all around her....

She began to weep then, galloping full-speed through the only world where, for a very, very long time, she had ever been happy.

Welcome Jean Krupa, World's Greatest Girl Drummer!

◯◯◯

Nobody remembers Jeannette Crupiti today. Even at her peak sixty years ago few knew who she was, though she was the best anybody had ever seen—and probably the *only* girl. Certainly the only one I'd ever heard of.

Search the reference books for "Jeannette Crupiti" and you're not likely to find anything. She was never famous—not really famous. She did a little TV, but in those early days there was no videotape and nobody at a little local station would have bothered to kinescope their broadcast of a band like the Skye High Five. There was a record, a 78 done in cramped little semi-professional studio, so badly recorded that Jeannie might as well have been banging on a bunch of old Campbell's soup cans as on the beautiful pearl-finish Slingerland kit she was so proud of, with the big "JC" crest custom-printed on the bass head. Cut just before the LP era began, that record, the only one of the Skye High Five, is a desecration; but not even the most fervent jazz aficionados know about it, as it was never commercially released. And so Jeannie's just gone, that's all, forgotten. As if she'd never existed.

And Boone Branson? His memory I buried many years ago. If I could somehow burn it out of my brain, I'd do it—even now my breath comes short and I start to shake with rage if I think of him, if I just remember his name. He's gone too, obliterated, but that's as it should be. To hell with him. I mean that literally—if there is a God and if there is a Devil, then Boone Branson should be screaming in fiery eternal agony right now and a minute from now and an hour from now and forever.

If he isn't, there's something bad wrong with this world.

○○○

But as I think about it I realize that there's a slight possibility Jeannette Crupiti might have earned a passing mention in some book on jazz. But not as Jeannette Crupiti. Not even as the cutely near-rhyming Jeannie Crupiti, which is what I'd call her on the tour bus to tease her, chanting it like a child: "*Jean*-nie Crup-*i*-ti, *Jean*-nie Crup-*i*-ti!" No, if she's ever been referred to in a book it would almost certainly be under the ridiculous stage name she got saddled with. It was never official and she hated it, never allowed it to be used in the band's publicity—but people used it anyway.

Jean Krupa.

Maybe now that the twentieth century is gone you don't know what that means. It's hard to believe today, when he's all but forgotten except by the old-time jazz fans, but once upon a time Gene Krupa—that's *Gene* Krupa, G-E-N-E—was the most famous drummer on the face of the Earth. Everybody knew who he was. With his dark-featured movie-star looks and incredible talent, Gene Krupa was the first really big-name drummer, a featured act with Benny Goodman and eventually with his own orchestra; sticks blurred with speed, hair flying, Krupa was something to see when he laid into "Sing Sing Sing" or "Young Man with a Beat." He was a showman, a *star,* the inventor of the thunderous, arms-flailing drum solo in an era when other drummers just held down the time and tried to stay as unobtrusive as possible. Hell, he was so famous they made a movie about him, *The Gene Krupa Story*, in the '50s. It wasn't bad. Sal Mineo played Gene.

Anyway, don't get me wrong—Jeannie Crupiti *idolized* Gene Krupa. But once Stan tagged her with the "Jean Krupa" bit in front of some reporters, it was all over. ("She's the female Gene Krupa—sure, fellas, that's J-E-A-N Krupa, how 'bout that, huh?") As sure as Joe DiMaggio was The Yankee Clipper or Erich von Stroheim The Man You Love to Hate, Jeannette Crupiti became Jean Krupa—World's Greatest Girl Drummer.

Sounds sexist as all hell now, doesn't it? Dazzled musicians used to come up to her after a set and, in all innocence, say things like, "You play like a *real* drummer!" But nobody thought of such stuff as sexism then. I don't even think Jeannie did. She was just happy to have a place in the band, happy to be playing; I don't think she ever really wanted anything else. I remember once in a hot little club in Baton Rouge, standing off to the side of the stage watching her finish a particularly long, fierce solo, just tearing up the kit, tearing up the audience—they'd never seen *anything* like Jeannie before—and at the conclusion, after her patented *swish-boom-boom-snap* high hat/bass/rimshot flourish that she typically ended on, she jumped off the kit, waved to the cheering audience and ran off stage in my direction. As she came up to me, breathless, face flushed, shoulders and arms gleaming with sweat, I noticed her hands and cried: "Jeannie, my God, you're bleeding!"

She stopped just a moment, glanced down at her two dripping red palms. "Shit, Lester!" she laughed, looking at me with her crystal-blue eyes and grinning in the lopsided way she had. "If you ain't bleedin', you ain't *playin'!*"

◖◉◗

Back it up now; take it from the top. Count it in. One, two, three...

I joined the Skye High Five in 1943, after Stan's original guitarist was called up for the Army. The same thing had happened with his bassist only months before, so he was desperate. Practically all the good players had been drafted, and the few who remained lived in fear every day of their notice showing up from Uncle Sam—that single awful page headed with the doom-haunted words, "Order to Report for Induction." (Of course, not everybody was afraid or unwilling. Plenty of eager musicians volunteered. Glenn Miller, the greatest trombonist swing music ever had, did, and eventually paid for it with his life. They made a movie about him, too.)

Anyway, by the fall of '43 there was a conspicuous lack of able-bodied young men around. You noticed it everywhere, not just in music. I was nineteen and 4-F; considering the runt I was (five-two on a good day, 115 pounds, glasses with lenses thick as the bottoms of Coke bottles), there was never much chance any branch of the service would want to have a fool thing to do with me. It was a relief but also a kind of burden, for by the autumn of 1943 if you were young, male, and capable of forward locomotion, you were supposed to be off fighting Hitler or Hirohito, not sitting in your bedroom trying to find the chords to play along with Artie Shaw on a radio broadcast of "Interlude in B-flat." 4-Fers were looked at with suspicion and hostility, though at least with my height and weight and bad vision I had obvious reasons for not being allowed in the war effort. Somebody like Sinatra, 4-F because of a perforated ear drum, was in a different boat—people still loved his singing but in the war years you didn't hear people saying anything good about Frank Sinatra the man. "Coward," "yellow-bellied," "used his money to stay out of it," all that. (The bobby-soxers didn't care, but it hurt him. His career didn't fully recover until the '50s.)

I had no career, and at that point in my life few cared enough to bother to hate me, like me, or feel much of anything else toward me. I'd left home the previous winter, unable to face another desolate December in Lonestone, Nebraska, where my parents had a little farm. I wasn't much use as a farmhand; my father—decorated Army captain of the First War—ran what things there were to run and had little use for his jazz-crazed pipsqueak of a boy. My mother I remember mostly as a lifeless gray-haired figure in a rocking chair, sighing and drinking. The little house we lived in was dark, dusty, and silent as a sepulcher; I spent my time behind a closed door upstairs in my room, playing the band remotes that came on most nights on the little cigar-box Zenith radio I'd saved up for months to buy. It didn't have the sound quality of the big Philco downstairs but it was *mine,* and without my parents' doleful eyes on me I could sit on the edge of my bed for hours, listening and playing along on my old Harmony archtop guitar.

Once high school finished—I graduated, a source of no pride to Dad, who would have preferred to see me a foot taller and bayoneting luckless Japs—I knew I had to get away from Lonestone, Nebraska. I'd played in what passed for our school band (it wasn't much), but there was no possibility anywhere near Lonestone to actually be a musician, to make music my *life,* which is what I burned to do. So the day after graduation, guitar and stuffed duffle bag in tow, I hitched a ride to Whitegate, the nearest sizable town, and boarded a Greyhound bus that eventually connected to another which took me to New York City. Simple as that.

Long story short: things worked out okay. I went through some bad months at the beginning, living in a run-down boardinghouse in Brooklyn, washing dishes on the breakfast shift at Moe's, a nearby greasy spoon, and trying to connect with real musicians. I strummed my guitar for tips at restaurants here and there. Finally I met up with a couple of guys, a piano player and a bassist, young 4-Fers like me, and we created the first real combo I was ever in: the Brooklyn Batters. (This was when Brooklyn still had the Dodgers, remember.) We played pick-up gigs at weddings, at bars and low-end clubs around New York; but our biggest accomplishment was becoming the house band for some eighteen months at the Star Hotel in Bed-Stuy, just off Flushing Avenue. It wasn't glitzy, but playing night after night, learning the tunes people would request, improvising, tossing musical ideas back and forth with the other guys, turned me into a pro. We worked hard, put in long hours.

I got to know New York too, though I was shy and self-conscious about my size and so kept to myself on my endless jaunts to see the sights, to hear bands all over the city. I didn't really make friends, much. I also didn't get a lot of sleep in those days, but when you're young and hungry (I don't mean hungry for food), who needs it? The Brooklyn Batters made reasonable money, enough to keep us in hamburgers and cigarettes and for me to upgrade my guitar to a nice second-hand Gretsch Resonator. The band obtained some cheap uniforms, too—blue and white, naturally, like the Dodgers. We did all right for a while.

Well, the Brooklyn Batters up split when the bass player came into a little money from a dead uncle and decided to open a shoe store—would you believe it was still in business forty years later? I was at loose ends again when some guys at a club mentioned to me they'd heard Stanley Skye was looking for a guitar man.

"Stanley Skye?" I asked with some contempt. "Is *he* still alive?"

Skye had been big stuff in jazz once upon a time, but that time was long gone—his best-selling records ("Flaming Spear," "Heat Up the House," "Be With Me") had been back in the Dark Ages, the late '20s. I literally hadn't known if he was alive or dead, and until that moment I hadn't cared, either. People like Stanley Skye were dinosaurs from another era. Still, it represented the possibility of *work*. I'd quit the job at Moe's when the Brooklyn Batters were at their peak (such as it was), and at the moment I had five dollars in my wallet and no sure way of making my next rent payment. So I made a few calls from the phone in the boardinghouse's main room, finally getting in touch with somebody in Skye's band who said I should come audition for the man himself at a rehearsal hall in The Bronx the next day.

In that damp, dingy place Stanley Skye struck me as an exhausted old slob, though he wasn't more than fifty at the time. He'd put on a lot of weight since his glory years. His jowls sagged, and you could see he'd had his suits let out again and again instead of buying new ones. He smoked and drank too much, sweated a lot, and wore the saddest toupee I'd ever seen.

But he was still a monster player. Skye was best known as a trumpeter, but he was just as hot on a sax; he wasn't bad on clarinet, either. Little if anything had happened to his talent, and on that afternoon, once he'd sat bulging and seemingly half-asleep in a folding chair listening to me run through a few standards with a couple of guys in his group, he got up and, without fanfare, brought his trumpet out of its case—and *blew*. I don't know how many songs we did that day, maybe a dozen, but Skye was the first world-class musician I'd ever played with and as I just tried to keep the chord changes straight, the man burned those tunes down. We did small-combo arrangements of "Heart and Soul," "Take the 'A' Train," "Flying Home," and plenty of others. Sometimes he was on trumpet, sometimes sax. Loose, improvisational, just jamming, no pressure; whenever I asked him how he wanted me to play something he'd answer with the same words: "Just play, man."

Well, I must have done something right, because as afternoon faded into evening he finally began putting away his instruments, casually asking over his shoulder: "What's your name again, kid?"

"Lester, sir. Lester Russell."

"Well, you ain't the best I ever heard, Lester, but you ain't bad. What're you doin' for the next six months?"

My heart jumped. "Not—not a thing, Mr. Skye. I'm not doing anything."

He looked at me steadily for a moment. "So be here at nine in the morning tomorrow to go over your charts and run through the show. We got a gig in Queens tomorrow night."

◙◙◙

I'd been with the band for a year by the time Jeannie came aboard. We'd traveled all over the country, playing everyplace from third-rate hotels in Jersey and Connecticut to dilapidated blues clubs in Mississippi and Alabama where they were quite unaccustomed to seeing all-white bands— and not always that friendly about it, either. We made it around in a 1930 Model A bus, a grumbling, flatulent old kid-carrier that Stan had picked up cheap somewhere and which his men had painted with jazzy rainbow colors (to match our jazzy rainbow outfits) and emblazoned with the words "The Skye High Five!" on every side. We had no roadies, no assistants of any kind; the guys took turns driving, all except Stan and me (I didn't drive, and anyway my feet barely reached the pedals). Stan was his own business manager, taking care of arranging the gigs, getting us accommodations (sometimes pretty primitive ones), paying us—not much, God knows, but he was an honest man and what little we got came in on time every time.

On the rare occasions we weren't on the road—and they *were* rare, for we played no fewer than two hundred and fifty dates in my first year—Stan retreated to his home on Long Island, an immense place that, but for a couple of employees, he lived in by himself. His wife had died long before; he had no kids. The other guys had their own homes and families in different parts of New York, but when Stan learned that "the midget," as he affectionately referred to me, had no real fixed address, he invited me to stay at Castle Skye, as I affectionately referred to it. His generosity wasn't limitless— I paid rent when I was in residence there—but it was great for me: a welcome break from broken-down apartments in Brooklyn, certainly. Stan knew lots of people in the music business and some visited him—I met Lionel Hampton there—but mostly it was quiet, even rather bucolic. Stan's star days were twenty years behind him, but he'd clearly managed his money well and had no financial worries—a fact which fueled his quixotic attempt to get back into the limelight, something he deeply wanted to do. "I don't need a lot," he said. "Just a band good enough to play the top clubs again. Maybe a hit record. Just one. I mean, I ain't dead yet." To achieve these goals, or dreams, he was willing to live like any hungry young jazz musician, constantly traveling, staying

144 | Christopher Conlon

in bad lodgings and eating in bad restaurants. "It's what you do," he explained. "You build it up. It's what I did twenty years ago. And I'll do it again." In the end, he was a road warrior; he would always rather play a gig for twenty people at a broken-down club in the middle of nowhere than spend a night in his own bed at home.

Stan's support players were all former session men in their fifties and sixties, tired, seen-it-all guys far beyond draft age, good musicians but past their primes, relying on their technique and their old tricks instead of thinking up fresh ones. In addition to Stan and me, the Skye High Five consisted of three men: Freddie Freck, the pianist, a tall, whip-thin guy with a passion for gin rummy; Hank McMurty, the bullet-bald bass player who preferred chess; and Lou Morton, our drummer, a dough-faced, sad-eyed fellow who followed baseball like some people followed the Bible. I knew I looked like a child sitting up there onstage with them, as sure as I knew that if Stan had had much choice I would never have been part of the group; I was a fair guitarist, sure, but there were a hundred guys off in Europe and the Pacific Islands who were better. But I was young, which I suppose was really a plus, and I was eager. And I wasn't going to be drafted.

To understand how far all this was from the days of "Flaming Spear" and "Be With Me," you only need to think about how the band itself had changed over the years. A truthful billing of the group we had then would have read this way:

Appearing Tonight—

**Stanley Skye's
Skye High Five**

Formerly Known As

**Stanley Skye's
Skye High Six**

Formerly Known As

**Stanley Skye's
Skye High Seven**

Formerly Known As

**Stanley Skye's
Skye High Orchestra**

We were on the skids, all right. But for me, a kid from nowhere who'd seen little of anything in his life, it was all magical. The cities, the lights, the people—paying audiences every night! Applause—for me! Well, most of it, of course, was for Stan, but I was up there, sitting in my shadowy corner of the stage holding down the rhythm with Hank and Lou while Stan and Freddie (of course we called him "Fast Freddie") took the leads.

The Skye High Five never had a singer. Stan would take the vocal line on his trumpet or one of his saxes (he had three, soprano, alto, and tenor); even occasionally on clarinet. He had a special rack for all his instruments mounted on the side of the stage and sometimes he'd clown around during a song, pretending to be deciding which one to play next, looking at this one and that one, holding them up to the audience for them to vote their choice and maybe blowing a few notes before picking the one he knew he was going to pick anyway and then proceeding to knock their ears out. Good music, good showmanship.

One night we were in a small seaside club in Pismo Beach, California, a little town quite a long way north from L.A. and quite a long way south from San Francisco, the cities we would have been playing if we'd been more successful then. Called The Beachcomber, it did a brisk business exactly because it was so far from any real center of music—a long way even from, say, Santa Barbara—so the club got all the hungry jazz hounds from thirty miles in every direction, serving up good steaks and good martinis in a casual atmosphere. We were booked there for two weeks, staying at the local motel, playing eight p.m. to two a.m. every night but Monday. It wasn't bad, and was pretty typical, I guess, of the kinds of gigs we were getting in that period. Low-end, but still marginally respectable.

It was on a Wednesday night, past midnight—the place was pretty quiet, about a third full (capacity was maybe a hundred). On nights like this, when we weren't playing to very many people, Stan loosened up and we'd run through some lesser-known tunes, personal favorites, sometimes in what amounted to extended jam sessions, letting a song fly for eight, ten minutes, Stan and Freddie trading solos while the rest of us held down the groove. At that point we weren't too concerned with the audience—this was more for ourselves.

Well, earlier in the evening I'd noticed sitting over to the far right of the stage a young girl sipping what looked like ginger ale through a straw. There was nothing unusual about that, except that she seemed very keen on us, really watching the band, studying all our moves. There was no one with her. I wasn't paying that much attention, but I do remember noticing her from time to time and being mildly surprised nobody was keeping her company. There were some loose guys in the club, servicemen mostly, and now and then one of them would move hesitantly toward her but then turn away, shaking his head. I don't know if she was putting out an unfriendly vibe or if they simply realized as they got close to her that she was probably too young, but in any event, they left her alone.

You could see she was into the music. She leaned forward, elbows on the table, eyes not leaving the stage for a second. She was pretty, in a tomboy sort of way: dirty blonde hair that reached loosely to her shoulders, no treatment at all—no styling, not even a simple wave, just free in a way only very young girls would feel comfortable with; grown women wouldn't wear their hair in public like that for another twenty years. She had on a white blouse, none too clean, with a bright red scarf around her neck and a pretty damn short white pleated skirt that showed her legs—legs without any stockings, which added to the effect of her youth. She chewed gum as vigorously as any bobby-soxer between sips at her straw.

But what I really noticed was that both her feet were tapping in time to every song. Not just the basic 4/4 that anybody taps their feet along to a song with, but the actual specific rhythm of each number—her feet, wrapped in plain black sandals, were mimicking perfectly what Lou was doing

on the bass drum and high hat. 5/4, 7/8, it didn't matter. She
had them all perfectly. Her head bobbed lightly with the
rhythm and sometimes she'd quietly tap the table with her
fingers as well, not calling attention to herself or anything,
but again, she matched Lou beat for beat. You didn't see that
every day. This wasn't somebody just enjoying some music.
She *knew* the music.

During a break I was left alone on stage, restringing my
Gretsch's D string that had popped near the end of our last
number, while the other guys hit the bar or the bathroom. I
was tuning up when I suddenly realized that the girl from the
table in the corner was standing around the other side now,
near me, watching me.

"Hi," I said finally.

"Hi," she said, smiling, chewing her gum rapidly. Close up
she was maybe a little less pretty than she'd seemed, with a
chin a bit too prominent and lips somewhat thin and pale,
but her big crystal-blue eyes were beautiful and her smile
was adorably crooked, the right side higher than the left; the
smile revealed deep dimples on either side of her mouth, and
her cheeks were dusted with cinnamon-colored freckles. Her
nose was a little upturned button. She wore no makeup at all,
and this, along with the lack of stockings, created an effect of
her being essentially a child, though through the white
blouse it was easy to detect the presence of compact but full
breasts, and her skirt covered gentle but real curves. She was
short, only an inch or so taller than me, but looked very
strong: her shoulders and forearms were muscular, sculpted
in a way I associated with Ann Curtis or Gloria Callen,
champion swimmers much in the news then. I would later
see with my own eyes how she could rip through one
hundred consecutive pushups without pausing, but for now

she stood like an anxious little girl, hips twisting, hands behind her back.

"Like the show?" I asked finally, for something to say.

"It swings," she said. "Stan Skye's great."

I looked at her, liking her immediately. Her face was open, guileless, innocent. "Let me guess," I said at last. "Singer?"

"What?"

"I mean, are you a singer?"

"What makes you think I'm a singer?" She pushed a few unruly strands of hair out of her eyes.

"Well, you're obviously a musician." I explained what I'd observed about her toe-tapping. "I just figured you must be a singer." After all, few females were in the lineups of jazz bands in those days. The only role for a woman was generally as the vocalist. "And you seem to have a nice voice." She did: it had a slightly hoarse, husky quality, quite pleasant to the ear.

"Oh no," she said. "I ain't a singer."

The guys were filtering back onstage. Lou came over, said hi to her. "What's your name, sweetie?" he asked.

"Me? I'm Jeannette. Jeannette Crupiti."

"Well, nice to meet you, Jeannette Crupiti."

"You're a good drummer," she said.

"Well, thank you. We were watching you from the bandstand. You a singer?"

She looked from one to the other of us and laughed. "You both said that. Does every girl have to be a singer?"

"Well," Lou said, "you must do *something* in music. How about these drums?" he said teasingly, taking the sticks in his hands. "Want to play these?"

The excitement in her eyes was obvious; they *glowed*. "Could I?"

"Well, sure, I guess," he said, slightly surprised. "You could sit in." He leaned close to her. "Know how to hold the sticks, honey? Here, I'll show you."

"I know how, thanks!" She took them quickly, adjusted the left one so that it rested between her second and third fingers and then did a quick, smooth roll on the wooden edge of the stage. She looked up at us and grinned.

"Wow, somebody's had a few lessons," Lou said, humoring her. "You want to sit behind the kit?"

"*Would* I!" Jeannette Crupiti fairly leapt up the steps to the stage, looked at Lou's banged-up old drum set with something like genuine hunger. "Are you sure it's okay?"

"Sure it is," Lou said. "Bang around a little if you want. But not too loud, okay?"

"Ha!" With that she dropped down on Lou's drum stool, took a moment to adjust herself, and then punched into a laid-back 7/8 beat, heavy on the bass drum. She only had to play for half a minute before anyone who was paying attention realized that she was good. She manipulated the high hat well, did clean quick rolls on the snare, highlighted tastefully with the toms and cymbals. It was smooth.

After a minute or two she stopped and looked at Lou and me. "Hey, thanks," she said, starting to stand. "I better let you guys get back to playin'."

"Hold on a minute."

Stan had returned. He stood at the front of the stage looking at the girl. "Who are you, little lady?"

"My name's Jeannette. Jeannette Crupiti."

"Jeannette Crupiti." He seemed to consider it while he lit a cigarette. "What is that, Italian?"

"I dunno. Just American, I guess."

He smiled. "Well, you were sounding pretty good there, Jeannette Crupiti."

"Oh, gosh, thanks, Mr. Skye." I could see her breath was coming fast.

Lou interjected, "I told her she could sit in if she wanted, Stan."

"Yeah, that's good," Stan said. "What do you say, little lady? Want to play with us a bit?"

She grinned and then nodded as eagerly as I've ever seen a human being nod about anything.

"All right, then, let's do it." The band reassembled. Lou sat off to the side while Stan ground out his cigarette and he and Jeannette conferred about what to play. Then our leader announced, "Gentlemen, the lady says she can play 'Heat Up the House.' Can't say she don't have balls." He looked back at her. "You sure you can handle it?"

The grin on her face as wide as it could be. "I can try!"

She leaned down and, to my surprise, slipped off her shoes. She was going to play Lou's pedals completely barefoot. Her toenails, I noticed, were unpainted.

But I was concerned for her. "Heat Up the House" is about hot as jazz gets, very fast and very complex. Hesitate for a second and the damned thing just plows right over you. I knew *we* could do it, but I suspected the girl would quickly get in over her head with all the lightning-fast time changes in the thing. I wished she'd chosen a simple ballad, something she could just sit back with and lay down a basic slow beat for, so as not to embarrass herself. Well, if she got into trouble I knew Stan would switch us over to something easy, a basic 4/4 blues or something like that, something almost anybody could play. He often let amateurs sit in and was good about covering them like that.

But "Heat Up the House" was her request, so Skye counted it in. One, two, three...

BOOM!

Right from the first beat Jeannette Crupiti was all over that fast, frenzied tune, slugging out a ferociously heavy bass drum rhythm while whipping the high hat violently and punctuating everything with rimshots and sudden rolls on the snare in places they didn't belong, no, didn't belong until she *put* them there and then you knew they had to stay there forever. Her eyes gleamed, she grinned and grimaced, her hair flew in all directions, her sticks danced, and there wasn't one person in that club, Stan Skye included, who had ever seen anything like it this side of Gene Krupa. "Heat Up the House" has a wildly complicated melodic line, which Skye of course nailed perfectly on his trumpet, but what was crazy was how Jeannette Crupiti's drumming not only held us all together but actually talked to Stan's horn, responding instantly to what he was laying down with triplets, rolls, cymbal crashes, fancy jabs on the snare, until it was obvious that the trumpet wasn't singing a solo at all, as it usually did on this number. Instead it was in a duet, a dance, a duel, a fight to the death with those damn drums.

Oh, it was sloppy as hell. Jeannette didn't know our arrangement and wasn't used to the kit; we were all thrown off balance by the power and volume of her playing; but that made no difference. The *feel* was there in a way I'd never experienced with a group in my life. With Jeannette Crupiti on drums it was as if the whole band was lifted to another level and she held us up there by sheer force of will, until finally after a long jam Stan signaled for us to close it up. We banged out the last notes, stretching them like licorice right to the breaking point, Stan's trumpet skipping and chuckling, Jeannette's drums barking and thundering in reply...and then it was over.

And the place, I kid you not, was dead silent.

Now, understand: it was late, yes, and this was just a little club in the middle of Nowheresville. But there were at least thirty people in the room. Yet you would never have known it from the sound after the band finished. Hear a pin drop? Hell, you could've heard a butterfly scratch its scrotum. Everybody just *sat* there.

Finally, from somewhere near the back, somebody said, very quietly: "Good *Lord.*"

And then all hell broke loose. People applauded, cheered, waved, stomped their feet. All of us, the whole band, just looked at the girl panting behind those drums and we clapped for her like hell, Stan most of all. She just smiled and breathed, once lifting her arm and waving to the crowd for a second, nodding to us, pushing the hair off her face, looking a little embarrassed. The only thing I felt bad about was poor Lou Morton, sitting disconsolately over there in the shadows, drinking whiskey. Lou was a good drummer, but he'd just been smoked on his own kit in front of everybody. And, insanely, by a *girl.*

I had a feeling, as I clapped my hands and watched the folks in the small crowd yelling their approval for what we'd just laid down with Jeannette Crupiti, that things were about to change for the Skye High Five.

I couldn't have been more right.

○|○|○

Stan couldn't just hire her on the spot, of course. We'd never even seen this barefoot girl before, and we already had a drummer. But there was no question at the end of the night that, if she was available, some talks would have to happen. She sat in for song after song, showing that she was just as good at being subtle and slinky (and *quiet*) on a ballad, all eerily beautiful little taps and splashes and ghost notes played with brushes, as she was wild and wooly and deafening on our hottest numbers. There didn't seem to be anything she couldn't play. At one point Fast Freddie started off the melody for a Duke Ellington mid-tempo blues, making eye contact with Jeannette with an expression that said, *How 'bout this one?* She nodded encouragingly to him and replied, "I don't know it, but just play—I'll catch up." And she did. She listened for a few bars, then just slipped right into the groove with her high hat and toms. Smooth drumming, loose, easy, right on the beat. Technical perfection? Nope. But anybody who tells you that jazz is about technical perfection is a fool. Jazz is about the rhythm, the mood, the vibe. And that's what Jeannette Crupiti had, like no one I'd ever heard.

At the end of the night we all sat around a couple of tables with drinks while they cleaned up around us.

"So where you from, kid?" Stan asked her, firing up a Lucky Strike. "Around here?"

"Here? No, not really. But I been stayin' around here lately."

"You sound kind of Midwest."

"Yeah. Maybe."

He smiled a little. "Where you learn to play like that?"

She shrugged. "Just picked it up, I guess."

"Honey," Freddie interjected, "nobody just *picks up* playing like that."

"Well, I had a little kit back home. I must have practiced 'Heat Up the House' a million times. It's my favorite record of yours, Mr. Skye. That's why I'm good at it."

"Stan."

"Huh?"

"Call me Stan."

"Oh." She grinned, and I noticed again how charming her face became when she did it, the right side squinching up higher than the left and dimples impressing themselves in each cheek. "Wow. Okay...'Stan.'" She sipped at her ginger ale and I noticed that her body was vibrating a little—glancing down I saw that her feet were quietly tapping out a beat under the table. Sometimes her head bobbed or her fingers tapped on the table to some rhythm in her head, too. It's a habit young drummers have. They can't sit still.

"And this is Freddie, this is Hank, and the midget with the glasses here is Lester."

"Hi," she said, looking at each one of us. "You guys sound great. You're such a great band."

Stan studied her. "How old are you, kid?"

"Me? I'm twenty-one."

He smiled and shook his head. "Try again."

"Okay, I'm eighteen. Just had my birthday."

(Of the many untruths and evasions Jeannette Crupiti laid down in our early encounters with her, this one was the most significant: we'd learn later that while it was true she'd just had a birthday, it wasn't her eighteenth but her *six*teenth. In 1944, though, few club owners checked IDs much, especially in out-of-the-way places, and rarely with the paid entertainers. I looked as young as she did and I'd never once been carded.)

As if to change the subject, Jeannette leaned toward Stan's pack of Lucky Strikes and said, "Mind if I bum one?"

"Sure." He held the pack out to her. She took one and he lit it for her.

"Thanks," she said, exhaling smoke.

"So tell us who you've played with, kid," Stan said.

"Me? I haven't really played with anybody. I mean, there was an all-girl group I was part of for a while. The Dixieland Honeys. Every heard of 'em?"

"Don't think so."

"I knew you wouldn't have."

"Mm." I could see Stan's mental wheels turning. "You married?"

"Me? Nah."

"Live with your parents?"

"Nah."

"Just on your own, at your age? Brothers, sisters?"

She shrugged. "Got a cousin, my cousin Boone. I call him Boonie. We traveled together for a while. But he got drafted. He's in the army now. In Europe."

"You get by okay?"

"Yeah, I guess so. I work at restaurants and stuff like that. Waitress. Or in the kitchen. Work one place, get bored, move on, work at another place. That's why I'm here now—I wash dishes at a joint a couple miles up the road. And Boonie sends me money sometimes."

"Hm." He scowled, looking long and hard at her. "We're here through the weekend. You be here tomorrow night, kid? Sit in on a few more numbers?"

Her eyes widened. "If I can sit in, you *bet* I'll be here!"

He glanced down at the black sandals on her feet. "So do you know how to play *with* shoes on?"

"Nope. I learned barefoot. I've always played barefoot."

"Shit," Stan chuckled. There was a long pause while he finished his cigarette. Finally, looking around the table, he said: "Hey, where's Lou?"

None of us had noticed that our erstwhile drummer hadn't joined us.

◎◎◎

Lou tried to hang in, but by the fourth night it was so obvious that Jeannette Crupiti belonged in the Skye High Five that he quit the group, selling his drums to Stan for ten dollars and telling us he was retiring from music. He disappeared in the middle of the night and none of us, so far as I know, ever saw him again.

Hey, it happens. When he'd joined a few years before it was because the previous drummer had just been fired. Lou had a wife somewhere in Nassau County and I imagine he went back to her. So be it.

There would have been discussions, of course. Stan would have wanted to know if Jeannette Crupiti would really be up for life on the road, if she could handle being in a tour bus day after day with a bunch of old men (the midget excepted, of course), and if she wouldn't get homesick. He would have asked her more about her family, her background. He would have discussed the practicalities of being the only female in a group of men that essentially lived together much of the time. He would have had her sign a contract, probably six months to start (unaware, of course, that she was too young to sign legal documents—she later showed me the convincing fake i.d. she carried around with her). But I wasn't present for any of this. All I know is that in short order Stan announced to us that young Miss Crupiti, rather than simply being a fill-in for the absent Lou, would henceforth be the official drummer for the Skye High Five.

Having a girl drummer was a hell of a novelty, but her gender, and to a lesser extent her age, presented some problems. First, we didn't have an outfit for her. She couldn't just wear one of the regular men's suits, though she did try one of mine on and we all thought she looked cute as hell in it. Still, our leader's wisdom prevailed: "Kid, you go onstage in that and people won't be talkin' about Stan Skye's new girl drummer, they'll be talkin' about how I'm hirin' *dykes* now." For the first few gigs she just wore her regular clothes, which looked odd—but then having a female sitting back there on the traps was going to look odd anyway, no matter what we did. Her obvious youth combined with my own made a strange visual separation—a jazz combo with three old guys and two kids, one of them a freckle-faced girl? When we took the stage at some of those early gigs people openly laughed at us. But once we started playing, they stopped laughing.

Finally Stan marched her off to a tailor who put together a proper rainbow outfit for her, splashy jacket with a mid-length skirt. He made her wear stockings too, though she complained (reasonably enough) that her barefoot playing would wear through them in no time, as indeed it did—keeping Jeannette Crupiti in stockings during wartime would prove an ongoing problem, but she absolutely would not play with shoes on. ("I *can't.*") He had her pin her hair up in some kind of arrangement besides what he called her "mop top," and that helped to keep it from falling in her eyes and made her look a little more formal.

"Well, you still look like a kid," he said, "but at least you're a kid that's dressed right."

But the key was our *sound,* and Jeannie—we were all calling her "Jeannie" within a few days of her joining us—quickly became the core around which we began to rebuild our old numbers. She didn't read music, which—given her abilities—was a bit of a shock to us, but it made no difference—with Jeannie it would always be, "Just play it and I'll catch up," and she was able to get her parts down faster than most drummers who spent their time studying charts. A bit more of a difficulty was that she knew little musical terminology; in our first rehearsals Stan would say something like, "Kid, give us a 7/8, okay, to bring us in on this," and she'd look at him blankly. Instead one of us would have to mouth the beat we needed from her, and boom, there it was, perfect. Nor did she have any idea of musical keys—A, B, G flat, it was all the same to her. But with drummers that doesn't matter too much.

Once we adjusted to her lack of technical knowledge, though, rehearsals were a dream; her energy, her enthusiasm, her *pizazz* gave us all a kick in the pants. Her playing style was very different from Lou's, much heavier, with a reliance on her thundering bass drum for the core rhythm—*boom-b-BOOM, boom-b-BOOM*—instead of the more typical high hat. This changed our sound, made it more driving and aggressive. Hank and Freddie were playing like I hadn't seen them do before, and Stan, if anything, was pushing himself in ways he probably hadn't since his heyday. Part of it was musical, yes, but I realized too that part of it was straight up *mano-a-mano* competition, each of them trying to impress the pretty young female of the species who was suddenly so improbably amongst us. At times they all but pounded their chests Tarzan-style to impress her.

But Jeannie didn't need any impressing. You could see from her face and hear from the things she said that this was all like a fantasy made real for her; she simply *loved* playing music, and to be doing it in Stan Skye's band was amazing to her. At first she simply followed along with what Stan said, but as she relaxed into her role in the band she started making suggestions—why don't we put the break here, why don't we add a chorus there, let's bring Hank up high on this lick—and often they represented damn good ideas.

Adding Jeannette Crupiti to the lineup also represented a considerable extra expense. Up till then the standard arrangement had been that Stan got his own room while the four of us shared two. But in 1944 it would have been impossible to have Jeannie sharing a room with any of us, so that meant the three men—Hank, Freddie, and me—got pushed together into a single room, which wasn't always terribly comfortable. But by then we were all in love with her so we didn't mind, not really.

When I say "in love with her," don't get me wrong. I don't doubt that the guys all had a bit of a crush on her at first; it's tough for an all-male group to suddenly be living with a cute young lady, sharing food with her, bumping up against her when you're getting on the bus, hearing her voice all the time, watching her change out of a jacket or pull her stockings up her legs, smelling her—especially on the bandstand, when she would start to work up a sweat. (We didn't know what "pheromones" were back then, but she sure put them out.) Yet their initial infatuation faded away quickly enough, and she became...well, Jeannie herself worded it best one night after a show when Hank shooed away a guy who was showing interest in her.

"Jesus," she laughed, "it's like having four big brothers!"

Then she glanced at Stan and corrected herself. "No, not four big brothers. Three big brothers and a *dad*."

We *were* protective. That's just the way the thing grew. Jeannie became our brilliantly gifted little sister, with all the protection and patronizing that implies. We never patronized her *music*—every one of us respected the hell out of her as a musician and knew the band had been transformed by her talents. No, it was offstage, once the playing was done, that all of us, even five-two 4-F Lester Russell, watched out for her, kept the randy young men at bay. Not that Jeannie really needed the protection—she was tough, and although she was close-mouthed about her past you could tell she'd been through some things. She was the first female I'd ever known who cursed—really cursed, like only working-class men did in those days. Words like "shit" and even "fuck," very uncommon then and unheard of in mixed company, popped out from her lips as easily as bubble-gum bubbles.

And she could handle herself. I remember one night after a gig in some broken-down club in the South Freddie and I turned a corner in a back hall on our way to the bathroom and came upon Jeannie sparring with a couple drunken louts.

"How come you so good with them sticks?" one of them said, pointing at the drum sticks she was holding.

"Is it 'cuz they're like *cocks*?" the other said, and both of the guys laughed.

"Yeah. You good at holdin' *cocks*, baby? That why you're so good holdin' them *sticks*? They remind you of *cocks*?"

Jeannie leaned casually against the wall, chewing gum and holding one stick up near her eye like a gun sight, peering down its very narrow shaft and tiny tip at one of the men. "Well, I'll tell you what," she said, "this one sure reminds me of *yours*."

◻◻◻

Jeannie and I were natural allies in the band. She looked up to Stan as a hero—a slightly tarnished one after all these years, but still a hero—and had friendly relationships with Hank and Freddie, but they were all thirty or even forty years older. She and I were of the same generation, only five years apart (though early on I thought it was three), so it was easy to bond. She and I were up on current trends, styles, slang, and even music that our older band brethren weren't. The Skye High Five, after all, was a bit of an old-fashioned combo by 1943, '44, playing a style of dance-friendly jazz that was certainly still popular, but which seemed increasingly conservative in the new era of bebop, with the complex harmonies and syncopation of people like Gillespie and Monk—artists who seemed to be breaking jazz apart at its foundations and building it up into something radically, even frighteningly different. Jeannie and I were fascinated by the new forms, and tried to interest Stan in them: but his soul was in the swing era and he wouldn't hear of it, calling the newer stuff "shit played by spastics." On off nights, when we were in the bigger cities, Jeannie and I would often slip away at night to go hear some of that "shit"; the other guys never accompanied us, usually sticking to the hotel bar instead. But Jeannie and I were kids, really, and we had the energy and nervousness and drive of kids.

It pushed us together, and as a result I got to know Jeannie Crupiti better than the others did. I loved being with her; I'd been with the band longer and was, of course, a bit older, so I'd seen more than she had of the life of a touring combo. Everything was *new* to her, and her wide-eyed enthusiasm helped energize me. We talked endlessly on the bus, fooling around, giggling (sometimes about Stan's toupee, but *never* in his hearing); she'd steal my food, pull the socks off my feet, abscond with my copies of *Dime Detective* or *Captain Future*, pulp magazines I was always reading. She didn't ignore the others—she learned how to play gin rummy from Freddie and chess from Hank, who had a little magnetized chess set for traveling; she also spent time lovingly caring for Lou's battered old drum kit, scrubbing the drum shells, polishing the cymbals and hardware, changing the heads when necessary. But she and I became fast friends. We'd go to late-night clubs when we could, to check out Coleman Hawkins or Charlie Parker, Jeannie's feet invariably tapping out the rhythms; but generally our free time was in the day, so we spent lots of time tramping around the afternoon streets of cities and little towns everywhere from Oregon to Arkansas, Texas to Tennessee. Jeannie was always up for anything, from a milkshake at a Woolworth's counter to climbing trees together in a public park—a young girl anyone would love to be with.

But she wasn't terribly personal. I remember one early evening in some Midwestern town—an off-night for the band—we were strolling back to the hotel from a matinee at a second- or third-run movie house, a film that had put her in a reflective mood: *Casablanca*, which was a couple of years old by then, but neither of us had seen it before.

"I'm tired of black and white movies," she said. "Do you think pretty soon all movies'll be in color?"

"I don't know," I said. "I hear it's expensive to shoot movies in color."

"But you *see* so much more," she said. "Remember *Gone With the Wind*?"

"Sure."

"*That's* a movie. The screen is so big and the colors are so bright that everything just *pours* over you."

"You'd see more if you wore your glasses all the time," I said.

(When the movie had been about to begin, Jeannie had suddenly rooted around in her little white purse and brought out a pair of plain black eyeglasses and slipped them on. Noticing me looking at her, she'd demanded testily, "What?" I'd just shaken my head and turned back to the screen, smiling; when the lights came back up at the end, the glasses vanished back into the bag.)

Ignoring my remark, she said, "This was a good movie, though. What was it called? *Casablanca*? Good movie. Pretty good, anyway."

"I noticed you got a little teary-eyed at the end. When Bogart left Ingrid Bergman at the airfield."

"I did not! It was 'cuz the guy next to me was smoking. It was gettin' in my eyes."

"I didn't notice it."

"Well, it's true. I don't cry at *movies*. Real life gives people enough to cry about."

I glanced at her as we reached an intersection, stood waiting for the traffic cop to wave us forward. "What do you mean?"

"Oh, nothin'."

We moved forward, gained the sidewalk again. I noticed that we were approaching a drugstore on the corner; since we had nowhere we particularly needed to be, I gestured toward it and said, "Buy you a chocolate soda."

"Hey, Lester, you're speakin' my language. But I'll pick up my own check this time, okay? All you guys pay for me too much. You're too nice. Especially *you.*" She punched me playfully on the arm.

I shrugged. "What else have I got to do with my money?"

"Well, same here. Really, Lester. You even paid for the movie. I'll pay this time, okay? It'll be a Sadie Hawkins date."

"Fine. I won't argue."

We sat in a far booth sipping our sodas, Jeannie as usual bopping along to some beat that existed only in her head: her legs jiggled, her head bobbed. Other than us and a waitress, the place was empty.

"Jeannie, where are you from?"

I'd never asked her a direct personal question, and what I immediately noticed was that all her rhythmic activity abruptly ceased. But only for a moment. Resuming her head nodding, she said, not impolitely, "Why?"

I shrugged. "I don't know. We spend a lot of time together but I don't really know anything about you."

She smiled. "Well, what do I know about *you?* Where are *you* from?"

Fair enough, I thought. I told her about Nebraska, Mom and Dad.

"Mm." She seemed to think about it. "That's interesting."

"And you?"

She looked at me speculatively. "I have a question for you first."

"Okay."

"Promise you won't get mad?"

"Why would I get mad, Jeannie?"

"I'm serious. It's a personal question. *Very* personal. You have to promise."

"Okay, I promise."

"Cross your heart and hope to die?"

"Cross my heart and hope to die."

She glanced around the store to be sure the waitress wasn't near, then leaned toward me, looked at me intensely.

"Lester," she asked quietly, "are you a fag?"

"Jeannie!"

"I'm serious. Are you one?"

"You don't...you don't ask that kind of question, Jeannie."

"Why not?" She sat back and looked at me with her wide, guileless blue eyes. "I thought we were friends."

"We are. You know we are."

"Shit, you're *blushing*. I'm sorry. I didn't know it would be such a big deal. Forget it."

"No, it's..." I didn't know what to say.

"Let's talk about something else. Let's talk about Humphrey Bogart. What other movies of his have you seen?"

"Jeannie, it's..."

"Come on, Lester. Now *I'm* embarrassed."

An awkward silence ensued. I sighed heavily and, though I had no words for it then—did anyone?—I did something I'd never dreamed I would ever do, something that would only be given a name many years later. I *came out*. I did it by looking at the table and nodding.

"I am one," I said finally, in a murmur.

She was silent for a moment, just looking at me. Then she grinned and said happily, "I knew it! I can tell. I'm never wrong."

"How?" I said, shocked to the roots of my virgin soul that I was discussing this with another human being.

"I don't know exactly," she said, considering. "Just the way you are. You're not girly. It's just...the way you move, the way you talk. The vibe you put out. I dunno. The fact that we've spent all this time together and you've never once tried to grab me." And so, in 1944, Jeannette Crupiti may have first identified what would eventually be known to the world as *gaydar.*

"Sorry if you're disappointed," I said in a voice that was barely above a whisper. I was breathing hard, feeling as if by nodding once and saying three words, *I am one,* chasms had opened beneath my feet and I was dropping unmoored through empty space.

"Oh, Lester, no," she said quickly, reaching across the table and taking my hand. "*No.* I don't care. I think it's stupid that people worry about stuff like that. It's just natural. It's no big deal. It's fine. Really." She squeezed my hand, looking closely at me. "*Really.*" Her voice dropped. "Your secret's safe with me, Lester. I promise. You're my friend. You're my *best* friend. I wouldn't do anything to hurt my best friend."

"Well," I said softly, "it's all just kind of theoretical now, anyway."

She looked at me blankly. Then she got it. "Oh. I'm sorry, Les. I'm sure it won't be. Eventually." She grinned. "You're a nice-looking guy. Have faith."

There was a long silence. I was disoriented, unsure of where I was or why. A burden that had weighed on me for years was suddenly lifted and I didn't understand how it felt. Good Lord, after all these years *someone knew.* Someone knew and here I was, still alive, still on the Earth, which continued to revolve on its axis just as it had always done.

"Oh my God," she said, grabbing my hair and pulling me to her so that our foreheads were pressed together. "Now *you're* the one who's cryin'!" She laughed. So did I.

◯◯◯

168 | Christopher Conlon

Lubbock, Scottsdale, Spokane, Salinas; Jackson, Cape Coral, Pembroke Pines, Sterling Heights; on and on we went, rarely in one place for more than a couple of weeks, as often as not just a night or two. Small clubs mostly, run-down, dank, dark places that had either seen better days or had never seen any good days at all. The odors of cigarettes, cigars, stale beer permeating the walls, the carpets, our clothes. Dressing rooms with cracked plaster and broken mirrors—when there were dressing rooms at all; often we were relegated to the bathrooms, and Jeannie almost *always* was, since hardly any place had separate facilities for ladies. Stages that sometimes had holes in the middle of the floor, that rarely had any proper lights beyond a couple of glaring-white spots, that had dangerous-looking loose wires sprouting like whiskers from the walls, that were often so small that Hank, Jeannie and I would be pushed up against each other at the rear, with me doing my best to keep my guitar neck out of the way as Jeannie's sticks slashed away at her cymbals. The house piano (that being the one instrument we didn't carry with us on the bus) would usually be out of tune, sometimes with dead keys, and occasionally simply not there at all, forcing Freddie to play my spare guitar instead. Half the time at the end of the night Stan and Freddie would be shouting at the owner for the money he owed us while Jeannie and I looked at each other embarrassedly and Hank smoked cigarette after cigarette, making no comment. A few times the promised "hotel rooms" turned out to be one big crash pad at the back of the joint, where we were expected to sleep on the floor under flea-laced blankets amongst the cleaning supplies and paint cans.

It was ridiculous. It was awful.

It was the best time of my life.

Jeannie's too, I think. That twilight confessional in the café bonded us forever, and made me feel a particular kind of closeness to her I'd never quite felt with anyone else. I want to say that we became like siblings, but in fact I've never seen a brother and sister as close as we were in that period. After all, we had no one else; we were the only people our age we knew. We talked constantly. Laughed always. Finished each other's sentences. Ate off each other's plates. Took the Lucky Strikes from one another's fingers. Pushed each other and giggled and acted goofy. Gave each other private nicknames (she, for obvious reasons, was "Bombshell"; thanks to my love of French-fried potatoes, I became "Spud"). Onstage the Skye High Five was a single integrated unit; offstage, it was Jeannie and me. But the others enjoyed our relationship too, and saw, I believe, the value in it for both of us—for *all* of us.

When we were lucky enough to have actual rooms, if only foul-smelling ones in a dingy semi-flophouse, Jeannie and I would visit each other late at night, or rather in the early hours of the morning. We could both be jumpy after a gig, and she disliked always being shuttled off alone to her own isolated room. ("Just because we're in the same room doesn't mean we're gonna *fuck*," she'd protest. "Shit, I'll *marry* one of you if I have to. How 'bout it, Les?") But rules were rules in 1944, and we had to be careful in our nocturnal turnings— even the rest of the band didn't know (at least I don't think they did) that after my roommate Hank had entered his deep-snoring phase I sometimes snuck out and made my way to Jeannie's, where we'd sit cross-legged on her bed in the dim light, Jeannie in a nightgown or pajamas, giggling, playing cards, and whispering to each other like children. Sometimes if the room had a functioning radio we'd quietly play the band remotes which were all you'd really get at that

time of night. (On off-nights every once in a while we'd get to
tune into *Suspense* or *Lights Out,* which were real treats:
Jeannie would hug me and bury her face against my chest,
squealing during the scariest parts.) And we could be silly,
pinching or tickling each other like kids—when I grabbed
one of her cute little feet once I discovered not only how
ticklish she was, but how callous-covered her soles were. Her
palms were the same way, testaments to many long hours of
practice; even so, she still managed to open up her skin
sometimes as she played, occasionally needing a towel to
wipe streaks of blood from her hands or feet.

"Jesus Christ," Stan would say, watching her. "Would you
please just take it easy on those damn drums?"

She'd laugh and, as often as not, toss the towel at him. "I'll
take it easy when I'm dead."

One night after a gig in Henderson, Nevada, Jeannie had
stayed up a bit longer with the other guys than she usually
did, drinking, chewing the fat. As a result she was a bit bleary
when I knocked on her door at two a.m. She opened the door
silently, as she always did, and I stepped in.

"Hey, Spud," she said, adjusting her pajama top.

"Hey, Bombshell. You were great tonight. Really
fantastic."

"Ain't I always?" She smiled. "You were great too. We're
both great." She dropped down face-first across the bed.

"Cards?" I said, fingering them in my pocket.

"I'm sleepy," she said, turning and looking back at me.
"Can we just talk?"

"I can go if you want."

"No, sit here by me." She patted the bed.

I sat. "So how're you doing?"

"I'm great." She smiled and seemed to hesitate. Then: "I got a letter from Boonie."

"Your cousin?"

"Yeah. He's getting out of the Army in a while."

"That's—that's great."

She looked at me. "Yeah," she said carefully.

"What? Isn't it?"

"Yeah, it's just…" She turned over, away from me, pulled a pillow under her head. "I'm not sure what he'll do when he gets out. It's not like he has any job skills. I was thinkin'…"

"What?"

She looked over her shoulder at me again. "Do you think Stan would hire him? As a, you know, roadie? We could use one."

"Hm. I don't know. I'm sure it would be expensive."

"It *wouldn't*, though." She turned to me, still on her side, took my hand. "Boonie would work for practically nothin', I bet. Room and board, that's all. He's big and strong. He's a good driver. Wouldn't that be great, to have a real driver, and somebody to set up our stuff and knock it all down at the end of the night?"

"Sure, I think it would be fine. But Stan's the one you have to convince, not me."

"I know." She sighed. "I don't think he'll go for it. He's too cheap."

"But if he works just for food and a place to sleep…"

"Yeah, don't you think so? Isn't that reasonable? I think it is." She twined her fingers into my own.

"Well, are you going to ask Stan?"

"Yeah, I will. When the time is right. I'm just not sure when that'll be…"

I sat there for a few minutes, then realized that Jeannie had fallen asleep. I got up quietly, switched off the single lamp that was burning, and had reached the door when she said sleepily, "Lester?"

"Uh-huh."

"Come back, will you? For a minute?"

I made my way to her in the pitch-dark room, stood over her prostrate form. "What is it?"

"Nothin'. Just...just stay here a while, will you?" She reached her hand out to me.

"Well—sure. Okay." I lay down next to her on the bed. "Something bothering you, Jeannie?"

"No...nothin'. I'm okay."

"You can tell me."

She squeezed my hand. "I know I can. Nothin' to tell..." Her voice grew blurry and I thought she'd fallen asleep again, but then: "Les?"

"Mm."

"Have you ever thought of doing it with a girl?"

I breathed. "Not really."

"'Cuz, you know...sometimes it would...you know, people can do different things. I did it with a girl once."

"Did you?"

"Uh-huh. It was...interesting. Sort of—softer. You know what I mean?"

"Sure," I said, though I didn't.

"It's just that sometimes I get lonesome."

"I know. So do I."

"I ain't a slut."

"Of course not. I would never think that."

"It's just that sometimes I wish that things were— different. A lot of things. In my life."

"We're all happy you're just the way you are, Jeannie. Don't change a thing."

"Aw, Lester, you're sweet." She leaned over and kissed me on the neck.

There was another silence and again I thought she'd fallen asleep.

"Lester?" she said, quieter now.

"Mm."

"You could—pretend I was a boy."

"Jeannie, come on."

"I'm serious."

"Stop. Please."

"We could leave the lights off. And we could do it—you know, like boys do. I wouldn't mind."

"Jeannie..."

And for a moment, with her hands roaming over me and her soft voice in my ear, I almost thought I was going to lose my virginity in the most unlikely possible place, in the most unlikely possible way. I touched her in return, exploring her body for a long moment. But no: I quickly knew it was impossible, insane. And hardly what Jeannie deserved.

I kissed her on the forehead and pulled away, standing. "Jeannie, go to sleep, okay?"

"You're my best friend, Spud...."

"You're mine too."

"I love you...I mean it..."

"I love you too, Bombshell."

By the time I reached the door I could hear her soft snoring in the darkness.

◎◎◎

Despite the indignities of life on the road for a third-rate band like ours, the Skye High Five *was* making progress. Stan's name had sufficient nostalgia value in the music world to get us our small engagements, and when people heard how tight we were, they told their friends and came back for more. But of course what they *really* told their friends about was that crazy girl drummer old-time jazzman Stanley Skye had in his band now. And as the months wore on, the gigs slowly got a little better. (I remember a great gig in Memphis—we played twelve straight hours, five p.m. to five a.m., by the end of which all of us were punch-drunk with exhaustion as well as actually drunk on the free liquor provided to us; and we—or at least the two youngsters in the group—were also high on the "reefer" a patron had supplied us, the first we'd ever had, which while on a break we gigglingly smoked together in a broom closet. The Five couldn't have been sounding too good by the end of that gig, but we sure as hell enjoyed ourselves.)

Jeannie grew as a musician in this period—and as a showman, or showperson, too. Her drumming became more disciplined even as her stage presence grew. We'd left the seemingly awkward and slightly embarrassed Jeannette Crupiti behind—the one who would only wave once to the audience when she finished a dazzling duet with Stan, then self-consciously look away. She was comfortable on stage now—with herself, and with her understanding that she, along with Stan, was the main attraction, the reason people were showing up at our gigs in slowly increasing numbers. Lord knows Jeannie didn't need any help, but Stan would give her tips now and then about appealing to the audience. Eye contact. Smile. Stand up now and then. Don't be afraid to mug for them a little. Jeannie, a natural extrovert, took to it all with ease.

Stan rearranged us on stage to reflect the reality of our new drumming star. He brought her kit downstage, closer to the crowd, while he maintained a position stage right just a little in front of her, allowing the two of them to see each other more clearly and interact more dynamically. Freddie would be stage left with his piano, a little behind Jeannie, while Hank and I were relegated to the back—me on a high stool that kept me from vanishing altogether. Instead of watching Jeannie from a position beside her, then, I was now behind her—which I didn't mind a bit, for I knew full well she was increasingly who people were coming to see, and anyway, I could see her better myself—see how she played. I loved watching her, the remarkable grace and coordination of her limbs, the almost magical way her feet could create complex cross-rhythms on the high hat and that ever-booming bass drum (and on a less sophisticatedly musical note, I adored watching her little behind raise up off the drum stool when she smacked a cymbal and then plop down again). Really, at that point Hank and I had the best seats in the house.

Anyway, it paid off. The clubs got bigger, the accommodations got better, the money increased. We were still a long way from a really *successful* band, but we were moving up. And Stan, an old showbiz hound dog, knew how to take advantage of Jeannie's nascent stardom.

"Kid," he said one night at dinner—Jeannie and I frequently ate with Stan; he was a bursting cornucopia of stories from jazz's early days—"we got to change your look."

"My look?" Jeannie said, glancing up from her Automat sandwich. (It says something about how limited our success

176 | Christopher Conlon

still was that we were eating dinner at Horn & Hardart.)
"What's wrong with my look?"

"You still look like a kid, that's what. You look like a girl."

"I *am* a girl."

"Uh-uh." He shook his head. "You're cute, honey, but
those guys out there who come to the shows don't want to
look at a girl beating those drums. They want to look at a
woman."

"Yeah?" she said uncertainly.

"Don't you worry," he said, smiling benevolently at her
and chucking her gently under her chin. "Don't you worry
'bout a thing. I got a *plan.*"

And he did. Over the next couple of months Stan invested
a great deal in the band, ordering us new, less gaudy outfits
(they were blue and white, shades of the Brooklyn Batters)
along with a new—well, newer—bus, a sleek modern
number with far more space, a smoother and quieter ride,
much more comfort all the way. He paid some artist to paint
"The Skye High Five" all over this one as well, in a much more
professional way than our old 1930 school bus had ever
looked. He paid for some needed repairs on our instruments.
It was a good time to be a member of the Skye High Five.

But it was Jeannie who got most of the attention. One day
Stan announced that we were "gettin' rid of Lou's old piece-
of-shit drum set—it's time we had some *real* drums for this
girl." And, on her seventeenth birthday (which they thought
was her nineteenth, though by then she'd clued me in to the
truth of her age), with no particular fanfare, some delivery
guys stopped by the club where we were rehearsing in
Dayton, Ohio and dropped off a bunch of boxes—boxes
which turned out to hold a brand-new, *not* used, Slingerland
drum kit. It was gorgeous, top-end, like something Billy

Gladstone or Jo Jones or Gene Krupa himself would sit behind. It had a beautiful pearl finish and big shining Zildjian cymbals. On the bass head there was an emblazoned crest that read "JC."

Stan didn't stop there. One afternoon she was marched off by a couple of people from some clothing store and didn't reappear for hours—until just before the show that night, in fact. When she did, I at first didn't recognize her. She was wearing an elegant blue spaghetti-strap dress, very low-cut, with a white skirt, cut daringly high for those days, and stockings. She had on makeup—the first time I'd ever seen her wear it—but not too much, just a hint of lipstick and tastefully subtle shadings to her eyelids and cheeks; her freckles still shone through, adding a delightfully girlish touch to her otherwise sophisticated look. She wore a gold necklace with a pale blue gem. Her hair now consisted of big swooping waves on top and long sinuous strands on the side which terminated in loose curls at her shoulders—it certainly wouldn't fall into her eyes anymore. And, incredibly, she was wearing *heels*—honest-to-God black stilettoes.

She was almost indescribably gorgeous.

"I feel like stupid Alice Faye," she said to us, but she was smiling. "Is it all right?"

"You look like a movie star," Freddie said, smiling.

"Jeannie, can you *play* in all that?" I asked.

"Oh yeah," she said, moving to her kit and sitting. "We chose everything specially with that in mind. The whole thing is actually pretty comfortable. It's loose so I can move. We thought about going strapless on top, you know, but I was afraid it would fall down during a solo!"

"And the heels?" Hank asked. "You gonna play in those?"

"You kiddin'?" she grinned, kicking them off.

"You're beautiful, honey," Freddie said.

"Les?" She looked at me. "Am I? Really?"

"You are, Jeannie. Really."

"Great," she said. "Now I need to practice playing in these fancy duds—so let's do it!"

○|○|○

Thus the Skye High Five entered its glory days.

Stan was right—Jeannie's transformation had an absolutely electric effect on the audience, especially its male portion. Men of the era had never seen a woman—and she *did* look like a woman now, the makeover adding at least three or four years to her appearance—moving like that behind a set of drums, looking so utterly desirable with her sweat-slick arms and shoulders and hard-pounding muscular legs producing that astounding, earth-shaking noise. Audiences could not sit still with Jeannie slamming away; even with songs that weren't "dance music" they'd be on their feet clapping, stomping, cheering.

The Skye High Five began to be noticed. First we got a few write-ups in local papers, always with a photo featuring Stan and a very prominent Jeannie; then larger publications began to give us a look. After a particularly good gig in Durham, North Carolina, an article called "Jazzman's Comeback With Amazing Girl Drummer" was picked up by the AP and appeared in dozens of newspapers coast-to-coast, together with a sweet photo of Stan and Jeannie smiling with their heads together, the old former star looking for all the world like a proud grandpa next to his young protégé. When Stan mentioned to a reporter that he was thinking about the possibility of us making some new recordings (thinking more wishful than truthful at that point), the news even earned a tiny squib in the back pages of *Variety*.

Jeannie handled the increasing success pretty well from what I could see, even if she would complain to me about the need to get "dolled up" for every performance now. But her confidence grew by leaps and bounds. Nor did she brush aside all the newfound male attention she was receiving. Between sets I'd often see her sitting at a table with someone, always a different someone, who was buying her a drink, lighting her cigarette, leaning forward and making her laugh. Naturally I felt a few pangs of jealousy; for well over a year I'd been Jeannie's only friend; but I'll confess it only *really* bothered me on the occasions—there weren't many, but it did happen—when, late, she would disentangle herself from some man's arm and make her way over to me, whispering in my ear, "Lester, don't come to my room tonight, okay?" With a quick kiss on my temple she'd add, "Love you, Spud," and flounce away with the man of the moment. But what bothered me more than the liaisons themselves was the fact that I rarely ever saw the man again, and the next day Jeannie always seemed a bit down.

But such moments were fleeting in the busy schedule of an ever-more successful touring band, a band clearly on its way up. When we appeared in bigger cities we began to see celebrities making their way to our show, celebrities who, I guess, sought out the musical cutting edge in the kind of smaller places we still played. Charlie Chaplin, silver-haired and not at all like the Tramp, showed up one night in San Francisco; in an out-of-the-way club in upstate New York Orson Welles and Rita Hayworth somehow found their way to us. Broadway actors, radio personalities (Fred Allen came three straight nights in Boston), columnists, and—of course—other musicians, who'd begun to hear rumors about that old has-been Stanley Skye's hot new group.

I especially remember one night in Newark when the great drummer Buddy Rich, fresh out of the service and then in Tommy Dorsey's orchestra, strolled in with an entourage of about eight people, making lots of noise and throwing his weight around. Jeannie saw him right away and I could tell he made her nervous (Rich was probably the most technically accomplished drummer in the world), but after an uncertain start with a sloppy "Heat Up the House" she settled down and delivered her usual spectacular set. The audience, of course, went nuts, but all Jeannie could do was turn to me at the end and say, "Was it okay, Lester? Do you think he liked it?"

"If he didn't he's an idiot," I told her.

I saw the two of them talking near the bandstand later, Rich all big teeth and brash ego. I couldn't make out what they said except that Rich was nodding encouragingly, seemingly complimenting her on the performance. At one point they moved together up to her drums, and I saw Rich pointing out something to her, gesturing between her snare and high-hat. Jeannie smiled and nodded—drum lessons from Buddy Rich? in a phrase that the *Peanuts* comic strip would popularize ten years later, "Good grief!"—but as he kept on talking and motioning I noticed her smile growing tighter. I could tell she'd had enough of the lesson. I'd seen this expression on her face before; I suspected she felt he was talking down to her. As she slowly inched away from the kit he followed her, and finally they exchanged a few more words, upon which Jeannie tilted her head in a particular way she had when she didn't like something. She said a few final words that made Rich laugh, and after a minute he moved off, still grinning away, and left the club, taking his pals with him.

At the end of the night as we were packing up I asked her, "Jeannie, what did you say to Buddy Rich?"

"Oh, he wanted to go to bed with me, of course," she said, amusement and contempt filling her voice in equal measure.

"And you said no? You said no to *Buddy Rich*?"

"Les, you know how fast he plays? I mean, he's the fastest in the world, right? But it's not all about speed. I mean, he's great, but sometimes he just plays like...like a machine gun, you know?"

"So?"

She grinned impishly. "So," she said, "I told him that. An' I said I figured he prob'ly made love the same way."

◙◙◙

Throughout this time, our own bond remained strong even as she got busier, called away surprisingly often in various towns to do interviews or photo shoots with—or sometimes even without—Stan, let alone the rest of us. Hank and Freddie grumbled about this sometimes, but I was just happy for her—and I knew that any attention she got would reflect directly onto the band and increase our popularity. I knew I wasn't star material; I was pleased to sit in the semi-darkness at the back of the stage, patiently holding down the rhythm. (In my years as part of the Skye High Five I never played a single solo, and that was okay with me.) Yet as 1944 eased toward 1945 it began to seem that things were going to change. Part of this was Boone, the cousin she'd mentioned, whose arrival was apparently imminent and of whom I was jealous in advance, for I knew he would inevitably take some, perhaps all, of Jeannie's attention away from me. But part of it was something else.

"Hey," she said one night in her hotel room, unzipping herself from her outfit and stepping out of it, standing there in her slip. "What's up? You seem down in the mouth." She threw her sweaty outfit at me on the bed.

"Sorry," I said, catching it and tossing it onto a chair.

"Lester," she said, authoritatively, hands on hips, "I'll get it out of you. You know I will."

I chuckled. "I know."

"So what is it? Tell me while I change." She disengaged herself from her underthings, left them on the floor as she moved to the bathroom. She kept the door open while she leaned to the mirror and vigorously scrubbed away her makeup. "C'mon, Spud, let's have it."

"Well—I've been thinking..."

"I can't hear you over the water. Come in here, will you?"

I did. I sat on the side of the bathtub watching her while she proceeded with her toilette. After a few minutes I said, "Jeannie, it's just that—the war news is so good, you know?"

"Yeah, ain't it great? We're knockin' the hell out of those Germans. And those Japs."

"Yeah, well..." The news *was* great, and many were predicting Victory in Europe within a few months. This was a cause of celebration for everyone in our war-weary country except, it seemed, me.

She turned to me. "What, Lester?"

"Jeannie, what happens when all the soldiers come home?"

"Mm?"

"All the best musicians are overseas. They're going to come back. Including about two or three hundred who can play circles around me on the guitar."

She scowled, moving to the shower and turning it on, stepping into it and pulling the curtain shut. "Lester," she called to me, "Come on. You're a great player. We wouldn't be the Skye High Five without you."

"Mm. Once upon a time Lou Morton was in the Skye High Five too."

"What?"

"I said I'm not so sure about that."

She peeked her head around the curtain. "Stop."

"Jeannie, I'm not good enough. Not for a band like this. Maybe when I first joined, when we weren't as good as we are now. But the group's on another level today. Thanks to you."

"Does that mean you're mad at me?"

"Of course not. That's not it."

After a minute she turned off the water and pulled open the curtain again. I handed her a towel.

"Then what's the problem?"

"I'm afraid of being fired, that's what."

"Could you hand me my pajamas?" she asked. They were on the toilet tank; I didn't have to stand to give them over. She stepped out of the shower, tossing the towel on the floor, pulled on the pants and stood looking at me as she buttoned the top.

"I don't know what I'd do," I said.

"Aw, Spud." She stepped to me, pressed my face against her belly. The flannel engulfed me in warmth. "Don't worry about it. It'll be okay."

"You don't know," I said into flannel. "Stan's in charge, not you."

"Stan's not gonna fire you if I tell him not to. He knows whose picture shows up in the paper all the time these days, and it's not his, it's mine. He knows which side his bread is buttered on."

I looked up at her, impressed with her self-confidence. "I don't want you to protect me. It's just—I'm happy. I love being in this band. I love touring. I love playing. I love *you.*"

"Spud," she said, touching my hair affectionately, "if you're not in the Skye High Five then I don't want to be either. Period. You know what I need to do?"

"What?"

"I need to find my Spud a boyfriend."

"Jeannie!" I buried my face in flannel again, acutely embarrassed.

"I ain't kiddin'. You need some sweet guy to kiss and make love to. I can find you one. A lot of the guys I meet swing both ways, I bet. I can ask some of 'em. What kind of guy do you like? Short, tall? Dark, light? Manly? Girly?"

"*Stop!*" I shouted into her belly, horrified but laughing too.

"Things are gonna change for us, Lester. Really. For you and me. I'll make sure that they do."

◎◎◎

Something in our discussion seemed to have energized Jeannie, because only a few days later Stan had new posters printed up. I don't think the timing of these posters was a coincidence—I suspect Jeannie cornered him and insisted on a few changes. Anyway, he always sent out posters in advance for any gig we were scheduled to play, posters that contained the band's name, a photo, a list of the old hits, and blank boxes where the specific information about the engagement could be written or stenciled in. The old posters had simply announced "Stanley Skye's SKYE HIGH FIVE," but the new ones added a crucial additional fact to that formulation:

Stanley Skye Presents
THE SKYE HIGH FIVE
Featuring Jeannette Crupiti,
World's Greatest Girl Drummer!

In addition to this, the name of each band member, including mine, was printed under us in the photo.

"See?" she said later, laughing, waving one of the new posters under my nose. "I told you he knows which side his bread is buttered on. Don't you worry about a thing, Spud. You're a great guitarist. I don't care how many guitar-playin' servicemen come home. Fuck 'em. Your job is safe, boy, or my name ain't Jeannie Crupiti."

◎◎◎

We were in the middle of sound check one steamy summer afternoon in the otherwise empty Fairgrounds Casino Ballroom in Memphis, having fun with the light-hearted Fats Waller tune "All That Meat and No Potatoes," when Jeannie leaned forward, squinting to see something at the other end of the room. Suddenly she shrieked, leapt up from behind her drums and jumped from the stage, running between the tables toward the club's front door, through which a huge man had just stepped in, setting a huge gray duffel back down beside him. I couldn't see him clearly—the light was behind him—but it was obvious who had just entered the scene as Jeannie yelled, "Boonie, Boonie, *Boonie!*" and jumped into his arms, wrapping herself around him like a happy spider. They remained thus entwined with each other for quite a long time, the big man holding her up, all of us just staring and smiling, until finally she dropped to the floor again and led him by the hand to the stage.

"Everybody," she said, "this is my cousin Boonie! Boone Branson!"

We said our hellos, stepping down to greet this one and only relative of Jeannie Crupiti's any of us had ever seen. He was a gigantic man, at least six-three, barrel-chested, perhaps two hundred and fifty pounds. He was wearing a cheap brown sports coat (with a few darker brown stains on it) along with an open shirt and threadbare brown slacks. But it was his face I noticed most of all: thick, square, with beard stubble and deep pits everywhere on his cheeks. His complexion was dark, swarthy. His eyes were black and seemed oddly expressionless, though he was pleasant enough to all of us on that first day. He didn't smile—Boone Branson never smiled once in the time I knew him—but he greeted us politely enough, in a voice that was a kind of low-pitched gravelly grumble that somehow made me think of the sound a bullfrog makes. When we shook hands mine vanished momentarily inside his big hairy catcher's mitt of a paw.

We sat at a table and Stan ordered drinks. Boone Branson seemed uncomfortable, as if his chair was too small for him, and it probably was. But Jeannie was simply glowing, gazing up at him and holding his hand, pushing her face into his arm now and then.

"Ain't he *great?*" she said to all of us.

"We ain't hardly talked to him yet, honey," Stan said indulgently. He looked at the big man. "So you're Jeannie's cousin."

He nodded. "From Indiana."

"Indiana?" I said, looking at Jeannie. "Well, we just learned something."

"Oh, come on," she protested. "I told you I was from Indiana."

"You never told me," Stan interjected.

"Me either," I said.

"Well, there you go," she grinned. "Now you know."

"Bole, Indiana," Branson said.

Jeannie giggled. "'Bowel,' you mean."

○○○

At first, the presence of Boone Branson seemed not so bad. Jeannie was preoccupied with him, of course, but I understood; he was an out-of-town visitor, after all, and her relative. They went out together several times during our Memphis stretch, Jeannie showing him around the town— we'd played Memphis before, she knew many of the sights already—and she invited me along to prowl the late-night clubs of Beale Street with the two of them after our own gig a couple of times. Part of me would like to say that I disliked Branson from the start, that I sensed something terrible about him, but it wouldn't be true. He *was* a little strange— not only did he never smile, but his eyes seemed lusterless, without expression, and when he spoke, no matter what about, it was always in the exact same lumbering monotone. Still, though reserved, he wasn't rude to me and didn't try to keep Jeannie to himself. It didn't seem to matter to him what we did; he responded to everything the same way, with an affectless stare. Even the first time he heard us play, the night he arrived, he just sat there at his table, big duffel bag beside him, drinking beer and staring. It was impossible to tell if he was enjoying the performance or not. It was curious, but I felt no forbodings, no secret understirrings of the heart.

And it was interesting, in those first days, to know him, if only to learn what Jeannie had kept secret from us. It was difficult to get many words out of him, but it seemed that she *had* grown up in a place called Bole, Indiana—which, I gathered, was as dreary as its name suggested. The three of us sat drinking one night in the after-hours at the Peanut Gallery, a club on Beale Street, having just caught the end of Louis Jordan's jump blues show.

"So what kind of a kid was Jeannie?" I asked, smiling to her. She smiled back indulgently but said nothing; she was willing to let Branson talk about their early days, but she had little to add.

"Good kid," Branson said, draining his beer. "I wouldn't've recognized her now."

"You're how much older?"

"I'm twenty-four."

"But you two were close?"

"Yeah," he said in his monotone. "Music."

"Did you play music together?"

"Sort of," Jeannie smiled.

"She was better'n me," Branson said.

"On drums? Is that what she played?"

"All we had was drums."

"Really." I looked at Jeannie. "So that's why you took them up?"

She shrugged, sipping her drink and restlessly tapping out little rhythms with her fingers.

Branson said, "Pa had been a drummer in the Marines, so there was an old snare drum there. He taught her how to play it. She was good. You could tell right away. Never had a real kit, though. Just picked up pieces where she could. Pa bought her an old bass drum from a guy for a buck. Used to bang around on that snare and that bass drum all the time. Used a hubcap mounted on a fence post for a cymbal at first."

"What did your folks think, Jeannie?"

"Didn't live with her folks," Branson said. "Lived with us."

Jeannie frowned, nodded. "Things didn't work too good at home."

Branson said, "We lived down the street. She moved in with us when she was eleven. We was a little better off than them. Had a record player. She never stopped playin' it."

"Started buyin' jazz records in town," she interjected. Then: "See, Les, we weren't really poor. Don't get the idea I lived in a dirt-floor shack or anything like that. Our house was small, but my pa did all right, worked in town at the lumberyard. When I went to live with the Bransons, they had a bigger house. Boonie's pa was the sheriff of Bole. They were doin' fine. They had a big Philco radio, plus that record player. We went to movies in town, Boonie and me, you know—ten cents and we'd stay all day. *Air conditioned,*" she said. This was the longest speech I'd ever heard Jeannie deliver about her life.

"Now," she concluded firmly, "can we please talk about somethin' more interesting than this shit?"

◯◯◯

After some misgivings on Stan's part, Boone got the job as our driver and general assistant. It would have been all but impossible to say no to Jeannie on this, considering that the man was willing to work virtually for free and our ever-increasing tour schedule caused us to genuinely need the help. And he was, after all, just back from Italy, we were told, apparently in the first wave of demobbed soldiers who would soon be swarming the country. He was a rather slow learner, I thought, but within a week or two he mostly got the hang of how to set up and break down Jeannie's drums, how Stan's rack of instruments worked, and how to treat a guitar or a big double bass when packing them for travel. He took over the laundry detail as well. But his main job was as our driver, and that was a huge burden off Hank and Freddie.

"This outfit's starting to feel like a *real* band again!" Freddie enthused. He'd been with Stan a long time, through the highs and undeniable lows.

And having a "roadie" changed things for me, too. It *did* feel more professional, having someone to take care of small details—to go out and gas up the bus or pick us up some chop suey after a show—even if I was always far too embarrassed to actually ask Boone to do anything for me. I'd been on the road with Stan Skye for a year and a half now, but my conscience niggled at me that I should remain the self-reliant Nebraska farm kid I'd always been.

Boone Branson carried a gun, a small black pistol, which was often dropped casually into the pocket of his brown sports jacket. This didn't concern me in the way you might think; after all, the world of less-than-top-flight jazz clubs could be a rough-and-tumble one, and several times the band was playing when a couple of cops burst in and arrested somebody, handcuffing them right then and there. We wouldn't miss a beat. Branson had also become, in effect, our bodyguard, especially Jeannie's, and her obvious regard for him soothed whatever concerns I might have had. And he was a returned soldier, after all.

On the road Stan maintained his private room and Jeannie hers; the rest of us were therefore left to cram into the single other room we had. At times Stan would splurge for two rooms for us, but for the most part we were sleeping in a single or, at best, a two-room suite, with fold-out cots for the extra men. Roadie or no, we were still some way from achieving a glamorous life.

But late on one of the first nights when we were thus packed in, I was awake when Branson got up suddenly and, slipping on a robe, left the room. I somehow was not surprised when I heard voices a few minutes later next door, in Jeannie's room, though I did feel a hot pang of jealousy. They talked into the hours of the early morning, just as she and I often had in a hotel room or the band bus. But I knew then that our late-night talk marathons were probably at an end, at least until Boone Branson moved on. I couldn't compete with a cousin from Bole, Indiana, someone she'd grown up with and, I suppose, loved.

But Jeannie, given her rising notoriety, had had less time for me lately anyway. She would always be sure to give me a wink during rehearsals or to plant a kiss on my forehead at the end of a gig, but I sensed Jeannie moving beyond me at this stage—she was certainly not a star, not yet, but all the elements were in place. She was beautiful, unique, and charismatic on stage, the consummate showperson; it was all Stan could do to keep up with her. In this period she was working out new routines, designing solos that were not only exercises in volume and speed but actual structured musical compositions, with a main melody on the tom-toms she then built upon, expanded, elaborated fugue-style while the cross-rhythms on the bass drum and high hat held down the core and her superb left hand played a modulated single-stick press roll on the snare or else flew wildly across the kit. Then, when the solo had reached its explosive climax, she would begin to deconstruct it again, taking away each of the complexities and colorations one-by-one until she was left with nothing but the basic tom-tom melody with which she'd begun, and the solo would end. It was an amazing feat of musical architecture.

But she didn't neglect the theatrics. Of course she knew the basic drummer tricks like left-right crossovers and twirling the sticks in her hands baton-style, but they weren't enough for her. I remember her practicing one move incessantly, a way she'd found to smash her right-hand stick against the snare drum so that the stick would fly end-over-end five or six feet straight up in the air, only to drop back down into Jeannie's raised and waiting palm. This was a tough one and it didn't always work—sometimes the stick flew off in the wrong direction (occasionally landing on my head)—but when that happened during a gig she covered it superbly, just grinning in that charming way of hers and shrugging to the crowd with an exaggerated "Oh, well!" expression on her face as she quickly grabbed another stick off the bass drum. Sometimes she got a bigger cheer for that amusing *mea culpa* than when the trick actually worked.

○│○│○

But with Boone Branson in the picture I began to feel—just slightly—alienated from the band. Life was still fine, I supposed, and Lord knows I was grateful for never having had to put on a uniform to go get shot at in France or Germany or Italy, as Jeannie reminded us that Branson had. Yet, while the band members were all perfectly cordial with me, I felt no real connection to any of them except Jeannie. Our friendship had become the emotional centerpiece of my life. I was twenty-one, on my own as a pro musician in a real band, yet at heart I was still a shy, insecure kid with what was then truly a terrible secret.

I knew from rumors that a "gay" underground existed in many of the cities we visited, but the idea of seeking out any such thing (as Jeannie occasionally suggested we do) was so shocking that the very thought of it caused me to blush to what felt like the tips of my toes. A few times men had come up to me after gigs, perhaps just vaguely hopeful or maybe with gaydar as unerring as Jeannie's, but when they would make their hints, or sometimes just straightforward proposals, I all but screamed and ran away in blind panic.

As a result I began to rely too much on Jeannie, I suppose; to place too much weight on one friendship, as the young sometimes do. For a while it had been grand, God knows, but between her ever-increasing success and the ever-present specter of Cousin Boonie, I knew I was being sidelined from her life. And it hurt.

◯◯◯

I can't deny that Branson worked hard; he did a good job for the Skye High Five, at least for a while. He got us to gigs on time, took care of our clothes (which included getting the blue-and-white uniforms dry-cleaned), carried bags, picked up food, and learned to expertly set up our instruments on any stage. He would go about all this activity with an absolute minimum of spoken communication; never rude, never abrupt, but somehow giving the feeling that he wasn't entirely *there.*

Jeannie's behavior changed around him. After her first few days of unbridled joy with him she began to grow moody, preoccupied; she always seemed very aware of Boone Branson, her eyes following him carefully as he picked up Hank's bass to carry into the club or grabbed a beer to nurse while watching us run through sound check. It was easy enough to shake her out of her distraction; sometimes even a "Hey, Bombshell!" from me and a swat on her behind as I passed by would do it—and she was *always* transported by the music, by the playing, by working out how to swap solos with Stan during rehearsals or by getting the crowd to laugh and cheer at her antics during the show. And yet the presence of Boone Branson upset the balance of the Skye High Five. For all of his hard work, it seemed impossible to get to know the man; his answers to questions were mostly robotically monosyllabic, and I never learned any more about his and Jeannie's childhoods than I did on that early, uncommonly garrulous night of his on Beale Street. He never joined in on the late-night bull sessions with the older band guys about sports, politics, women; and he hardly ever spoke to me about anything.

All of us, of course, wanted to hear about his war experiences, but after a few general questions were met with responses like "It was tough," we all backed off the subject. I was sadly familiar—we all were—with the sight in many cities and towns of young men in wheelchairs, young men with missing arms or legs. You tried not to stare even when you noticed in the audience one night a man with a hook for a left hand or another with a huge patch covering much of one side of his face or yet another who shook violently as if afflicted with some kind of palsy. You didn't see such people in the triumphant newsreels in the movie theater before the main feature. But they existed. And there were lots of them. As a result, we backed off the subject of Branson's war experiences.

But I couldn't fail to be concerned by the way he and Jeannie were together. She took to disappearing with him, and we wouldn't know for hours where they were; sometimes she only appeared again minutes before we were to go on. "Sorry, sorry," she'd say breathlessly, hustling in through a back door and scrambling to gather up her band outfit. "Got held up." A few minutes later Branson would walk in through the front door in his usual old sport coat and usual worn brown slacks, order his usual beer, and sit as close to the stage as he could, staring, always staring at her, like, it seemed to me, a man in thrall to a mirage.

◎◎◎

In the middle of some night somewhere I'm awakened by voices in the next room. At first I think I'm dreaming, but no, Jeannie's voice comes through clearly. "What am I supposed to do on a break when a guy offers to buy me a drink? Tell him to go to hell? Boonie, would you just be quiet? Please? Would you please just *stop?*" she says, exasperated tears in her voice. And then Boone Branson's voice, too low for me to make out the words, only that it's that same unmistakable monotone. I glance at my watch on the nightstand: 3:30 in the morning.

◖◯◗

In memory I seem to be at the back of the stage in a hundred different clubs, and in all of them sits Boone Branson, dead center, just staring at the band, and in particular at Jeannie. He doesn't move at all except to drink his beer. He just stares. Every now and then I watch him to make sure he actually blinks. He does. But not often.

◖◯◗

I found myself worried about Jeannie, even as I was aware that my own jealousy might be getting the better of me. I tried talking to Stan, to Freddie, but they had no interest in what they saw as troubles between "the kids in the band." The Skye High Five were on their way up, and they couldn't have been happier about it. Neither could I, of course; and yet even they couldn't deny that Branson could be a problem. More than once he got into verbal altercations with patrons in the clubs we played. Once, taking offense at a guy whom he thought was ogling Jeannie a little too much, he threw a punch at him, knocking him across the table and getting himself thrown out of the place; he spent the rest of that particular night in the bus. Stan gave him a stern talking-to after that and things grew quiet again, for a while.

Unable to interest record companies in the Skye High Five—Stan's nostalgic semi-celebrity was a double-edged sword, getting us in the door for some gigs but also trapping us with him in the seemingly permanent category of "has-been"—our leader finally took it upon himself to book us a few hours at Genius Recording, a local studio on Long Island, with the idea of sending around the resulting disc as a demo to the big labels. Of course it was a thrilling day to step into an honest-to-Pete recording studio—I'd never been in one in my life—even as I was a bit shocked at how small and distinctly lacking in glamor it was. There were two rooms, the control room and what they called the "floor," which were separated from each other by a glass partition. The floor was nothing but an empty room with a tired colorless carpet, big drapes everywhere, and a few microphones, mike stands and cables. The room was so small that it was difficult to set ourselves up. During the sound tests Jeannie's drums were so loud that the engineer said nothing else could be heard. The engineer and producer came "down" (it wasn't really down) to the floor to put up sound-baffling panels in front of her kit, which had the unfortunate effect of making it impossible for the rest of us in the band to see her, and even then they still had to ask her to try to play quietly. Jeannie was irritated.

Branson, meanwhile, sat in the control room, staring at us expressionlessly through the glass.

Stan had decided on "Heat Up the House" and "Be With Me" for our two tracks, the idea being to remind record labels of his past while also demonstrating the edgy, aggressive new sound he'd created with Jeannie and the rest of us. We ran through the numbers a couple of times as a warm-up, and they seemed to sound okay; when we actually went to lay them down, though, something misfired. It just didn't feel right with Jeannie hidden behind those panels; we couldn't communicate with her in that almost telepathic way all of us had developed by then, especially Stan. Meanwhile she was constricted by the requirement to "keep it down," as the engineer had demanded. Jeannie was no more capable of "keeping it down" musically than a young puppy can keep from leaping and barking.

As a result, she simply didn't play well. She was competent, certainly; but what she laid down was not Jeannette Crupiti, not really. She might have been any decent drummer. It wasn't her fault, but it was a fact—and in those days, in that kind of little no-budget studio, there was no multi-tracking, there were no overdubs or retakes. You got what you got. We tried "Heat Up the House" several times, each take costing Stan more money, but in this strange cramped environment we just couldn't capture what we blazed through every night like clockwork on the bandstand. It ended with Jeannie crying, *"I can't fuckin' play like this!"* and hurling her sticks to the ground, storming out of the studio. I'd disengaged myself from my guitar and was about to follow her out when, of course, I saw Boone Branson there first. So I sat and waited. We all did.

It took a very long time. At one point I wandered to the door, which was open. It was a clear, bright day, and sitting on the curb at the far end of the parking lot were Jeannie and Branson. He had his huge arm around her and was leaning his head to her, obviously saying something. I could hardly imagine comforting words coming from his hairy bulk.

But eventually she returned to the studio, Branson expressionless behind her.

"Sorry," she mumbled, passing by all of us and wiping her eyes. "Can we do 'Be With Me'?"

We did. It's a ballad, much less reliant on the drums, and Jeannie got through it reasonably well in the single take we laid down. Then we decided to hit "Heat Up the House" one more time, and on this take Jeannie was sharp. It wasn't the best I'd ever heard her play the number, but it was solid and impressive, even if she was still hampered by the sound baffles and by having to not play as she wanted.

"Yeah," Stan said at the end. "That's it. That's right."

She came out from behind the panels, her expression made up of equals parts sheepishness and relief. She looked very tired. "I guess that was okay," she said.

But in the end it made no difference. When we got the finished record later and put it on at Stan's house, we were all disappointed; I was devastated. The tinny, swishy-sounding recording hardly reflected what the Skye High Five was about. The sound was high-pitched and distorted; Stan's trumpet was all you really heard clearly, that and some of the higher notes of Freddie's piano. There were vague thumpings of Hank's bass here and there. But Jeannie's drums sounded like children's toys, like someone tapping haphazardly on tin cans; her wonderful, apocalyptic bass drum was so muffled it sounded more like ambient noise than anything that actually belonged on the record.

And my own careful guitar stylings? They were completely inaudible. No matter how we adjusted the volume or tone, Lester Russell might as well have not shown up for the session at all. I simply was not there.

"It stinks," Jeannie announced when the record ended.

"Well," Stan replied, "don't worry about it, kid. We'll have more chances. Lots more."

◉◉◉

Tallahassee Junction, another late night, voices from down the hall, Jeannie shouting, "That guy in the *bar* tonight? I don't even *know* him! You're being stupid! Just *shut up!*" And the rumbling monotone that comes in response, the words indecipherable, louder than usual but no more filled with any identifiable feeling. Then the sound of something striking something else: a book slammed on a table, perhaps, or a fist. "Stop it!" she screams *"Stop it!"* A long uncomfortable silence followed by what sounds like a gasp, then an unidentifiable set of thumps, one of them quite loud.

I get up, I slip on my robe, I pad out into the hall and knock loudly on her door. The room suddenly grows silent.

I knock again.

Finally her voice, near the door: "I'm sorry. We'll keep it down."

"Jeannie? Are you all right?"

"Lester?"

"What's going on, Jeannie? Open the door, will you?"

"It's okay, Lester," she says quietly. "Everything's fine."

"But what's going on in there?"

"Nothing. Boonie and I were playing a game. Go to bed."

"A *game?* Come on, Jeannie, open the door. Are you crying?"

"No."

"You sound like you are."

"Go to bed, Lester," she says again, more insistently this time. "I mean it. Don't worry. I can handle this."

◎◎◎

My memory blurs. There are a number of scenes like this enacted over a period of weeks; quiet nights alternate with shouting matches. Sometimes Branson comes gruffly back into the room and drops heavily down on his cot while I pretend to sleep. Other times he's gone until dawn. In the daylight Jeannie and I don't talk about it. We don't talk about anything. Our relationship becomes strictly professional; the closest thing to friendship comes with the quick wink or kiss on the forehead she sometimes gives me on stage. We're together all the time, on the bus, in restaurants, in clubs, and most of all on stage, but I feel she's moved away from me. Not to stardom. To Boone Branson.

◎◎◎

And then, suddenly, it all ends.

Coral Gables, Florida, a storm-swept night in a dark, terrible hotel, cockroaches skittering along the baseboards and water dripping from the ceiling into pans in the hall. The gig, a one-nighter, had been all but pointless: with storm warnings everywhere and rain cascading down in torrents, people stayed home; we played only to a dozen or so locals. The power flickered. We all played badly, even Stan. Everybody was relieved when we reached the end of the only set we would play; the club, we were told, was closing on account of the weather. We repaired to the hotel across the street; I sat drinking with Stan and Freddie for a while in the bar until they closed that, too. And so I sat up in bed listening to Hank's light snoring. Branson hadn't even bothered to pretend to be sleeping here; his big duffel bag wasn't even in the room. I dozed unhappily for a while.

At last I was awakened by screams, Jeannie's screams. There was a tremendous thumping and crashing in the room across the hall. As I opened the door I saw that the manager already there, banging on the door as Jeannie shrieked, "Leave us alone! Leave us *alone!*" and Stan and Freddie

202 | Christopher Conlon

appeared in the hall as well, the manager shouting, "I'm gonna call the cops!" as if any cops would come in the middle of this veritable hurricane, and finally he used his key to push open the door only to be stopped by the door chain and Branson's deep *"Get out,"* until finally Stan stepped forward and simply kicked the door in, the chain flying into pieces, and standing there in the main room was Boone Branson in his brown sport jacket and old slacks with Jeannie on her knees in front of him, her nightgown in disarray, her hair bunched in his fist as she screamed and tried to pull away and he simply slapped her, slapped her again and again until Stan and Freddie and the manager and I all stormed the room and he closed his fist and punched her in the face as we tore him off her. Blood sprang from her lip as he elbowed Stan and Freddie away, pushed past me and lurched out of the room, the manager saying, "I'm calling the cops! I'm calling the cops, you louse! You woman-beater!" and Stan, breathless behind him, shouting, "You're fired, Branson, you son of a bitch! Get out of here now! You're *fired!*" and Jeannie rushing between the two of them and out the door, blood running down her chin, rushing to the back exit where Branson had just charged through, running to the door and holding it open and crying, *"Boonie? Boonie, where are you?"* and padding barefoot in her ruined nightgown out into the dark rain, calling "Boonie? Boonie?" while we all just stood there aghast, speechless. She wandered the parking lot, searched the band bus, looked behind the garbage bins, crying again and again, "Boonie? Boonie?"

"Branson doesn't have the bus key, does he?" I heard Hank ask.

"Nah," Stan said. "I never let that bastard hold onto it."

After a time Jeannie moved toward the door again, the door where we all stood. She said nothing, didn't even look at us as she came through the doorway. She was drenched. Her hair hung limp in her eyes. Her lip still bled. She had scraped her feet somehow and there were ugly red abrasions on her toes.

"He's gone," she said finally, in a little girl's voice. She wrapped her arms around herself. "Boonie's gone."

"It's good riddance, kid," Stan said, taking her by the shoulders. "It's good riddance."

"But Boonie's gone."

"Kid..." He seemed to run out of words. This was not a situation with any precedent for a member of the Skye High Five.

"You want to come into the office?" the manager said to her. "I got some first aid."

"I'm all right," she said finally.

"Well, I'm callin' the cops," he said, moving back up the hall. "I don't want that loony comin' around here again." He disappeared.

The Skye High Five stood in the dark hall, all of us staring at Jeannie and trying not to. It seemed a woman's job to help her, but we were all we had. Jeannie stared at the floor and I saw that she was starting to shiver.

At last I said, "I'll take care of her, Stan," and moved to put my arm around her soaked shoulder.

"You sure, kid?"

"Yeah." I tried to smile. "We're friends."

"All right." He looked at Hank and Freddie. "I'll go talk to that manager. You guys just sit tight." He moved up the hall and was gone.

I helped her to her room, closed the door. Her eyes had gone glassy. I stripped off her nightgown and ran a towel over her, then wrapped her in a blanket. I tended to her lip and toes with a washcloth and soap. Finally she lay down on the bed, her back to me. I watched her for a time, until I realized that she'd begun crying softly.

I sat on the edge of the bed, smoothed her hair, made little "Shh, shh," sounds for a while. Then I wrapped myself around her body, holding her tightly, determined to protect her always, protect her forever.

◎◎◎

Over Jeannie's passionate objections, Stan cancelled a couple of weeks' worth of tour dates of the Skye High Five and announced that we would return to Long Island. "For R & R," he said, chucking Jeannie affectionately under the chin. "I think we all need it."

Hank and Freddie went off to be with their families; meanwhile I saw little of Stan in the days we were back at his house. For the most part he was off in his study, voice going a mile a minute as he tried to set up future dates, negotiate future deals. It must have been difficult for him, knowing his comeback depended on the talents of a gifted but troubled teenage girl with an explosive emotional life. I know it wasn't easy for him to cancel those show dates. But Stan understood, like the sensitive stepfather he essentially was, that Jeannie had to have a break, even if he had no real idea of what was going on inside her. None of us did.

And so the days passed slowly, as often as not Jeannie and I having the place to ourselves. She was used to Castle Skye; like me, she had no other home when we off the road.

But there was little joy in it this time. Jeannie hardly talked to me, instead sluffing around the house at all hours in nothing but an old yellow bathrobe and slippers. Her lip healed. When the spring weather was good she would sit out on the back deck overlooking the lawn just staring vacantly at nothing, smoking cigarette after cigarette and drinking coffee. I sat with her at times, though we rarely spoke. Mostly I listened to the radio, raided the big fridge, strummed my guitar, read the papers...the Allies were swarming over Europe, liberating one country after another on their inexorable march to Berlin. I felt nothing about any of it, the events of the war as far away as whatever events might occur on the Moon. I'd only ever been happy, really happy, with the Skye High Five. Whether we would continue didn't seem to be up to Stan; it was up to Jeannie. She was literally irreplaceable.

Yet there came a bright day when her mood seemed to lighten, when she suddenly said to me, "Wanna take a walk, Les?" and of course I did. She went upstairs and slipped on a lovely white blouse and skirt, stockings, sandals, and a big white floppy hat, draping a white sweater over her shoulder as we made our way outside, wandering around the neighborhood in the cool breeze. After a while she took my hand. We just strolled aimlessly, silently. It felt better then, she and I together, better than it had felt since Boone Branson had entered the scene a month before. We made our way to the little shopping center, sat in the drugstore and had chocolate sodas as we used to, listened to Kay Kyser and the Andrews Sisters on the jukebox.

Draining the last of her soda through her straw, she said, "Lester, I'm sorry."

"You don't have to say that, Jeannie."

"Shut up. I do have to say it. I've been lousy to you. Well—I've been a bitch to the whole band. But especially to you."

"It's all right."

"No, it's not." She took my hand, staring down at the table.

"Jeannie, I think…I think we've all just been under a lot of pressure. How many days do we get off? I mean, until this break, we were working six, seven days a week, right? For months on end. It just…it just got to you. It got to all of us."

She nodded, not looking at me.

I knew I was entering dangerous waters, but: "Have you heard from him?"

She shook her head.

"I'm sorry," I said, though what I was sorry for was the fact that Jeannie felt bad; I was most emphatically *not* sorry that Boone Branson had apparently made his final exit. I remembered how we'd left all his ever-present duffel bag sitting beside the bus when we rode out the next day; Jeannie was too out of it to notice, and as for the rest of us, well, if the hotel wanted to pick up his junk and hold it, that was their business. As far as we were concerned, they could throw it all in the garbage.

"Les?"

"Hm."

"Why do you think people love each other?"

I looked at her downcast face. "What do you mean?"

"Why do people decide, you know, 'I love that person'? Why that person and not another one?"

"I don't know, Jeannie. I don't think anybody knows that."

She scowled and lit a cigarette. "I think it stinks."

"What?"

"Love."

"Maybe you're right. I don't know. I've never been in love," I said. "Except with you."

She smiled a little. "Sorry I'm a girl."

"Not your fault. I don't hold it against you."

"Thanks. It's just...I dunno. I don't understand what happens."

"Happens?"

"When him and me are together." She looked out the window.

There was a long pause. I watched the waitress deliver a toasted cheese sandwich to a patron at the other end of the restaurant.

"Why do you..." I struggled for the words. "Jeannie, why do you...?"

She sighed; I didn't have to finish it. "That's the sixty-four dollar question, Spud."

◙◙◙

She didn't say any more on the subject then; but we'd opened a door, and slowly, over the next few days, she told me more about her early life and about Boone Branson than I'd known in the entire time I'd known her. Something in her seemed to need to talk, even as the words came at times slowly, haltingly, hesitatingly.

"I was hopin' I'd left it all behind me," she said on the back porch the next morning, sipping her coffee. "But it follows you. I didn't know that."

"What does, Jeannie?"

"It." She scowled, adjusted her bathrobe. "Everything." I waited for her to say more. "You know how people talk about a new life? There's no new life. That's what I know now. It's just the same old life." She seemed to think about it. "Like all those servicemen comin' back. Are they gonna have new lives now? Are they gonna leave the war behind? Just forget about it? I don't think so."

"No," I agreed.

"It'll always be with 'em, I bet."

"Yes."

"That's what I mean. It's never a new life. The old one just goes on, that's all."

I waited. She finished her cigarette, ground it out in the ashtray, and sipped more coffee. "Like me an' Boonie," she said finally. "You know what, Lester? I just realized something over the past few days. I realized that relationships never really end. I mean, even if you move away, stop talkin' to that person, stop seein' 'em...it goes on, you know? 'Cuz it goes on in your mind. You remember that person and your brain goes over the memories again and again and thinks about 'em...maybe it changes 'em, I dunno. But after a while you think differently about the person than you used to. They change. Inside you. Your perspective. You see them different. An' then later you see them different again. That's what I mean: it never ends."

She leaned her head back in the chair and closed her eyes. "Boonie 'n me...we go back a long way, you know? His family pretty much raised me after my dad lost his job and left me with 'em."

"Where's your dad now, Jeannie?"

"I dunno. He took off to find a job. Like a million other guys. Left me with the Bransons and that was it. I liked him, my pa. He was a good guy. But he didn't know how to take care of a daughter by himself, not without any money and without a job he didn't. My ma died when I was six months old. There wasn't anybody else. Givin' me to the Bransons was the best he could do. I don't hold it against him. At least he didn't put me in an orphanage, you know?"

"So you grew up with your cousins...?"

She opened her eyes and stared at the fleecy clouds wandering above us. "Boonie's not really my cousin," she said. "I mean, he sort of is. His mom was related to my dad somehow, but they weren't brother and sister. They're like, I dunno, second or third cousins or somethin'. It was explained to me once but it all went over my head. Anyway, Boonie an' me are more like—distant relations, I guess. But we called ourselves cousins. Went to school together—he used to be my protector, you know? I got bullied sometimes."

She sighed. "Boonie used to be really sweet. He carried my books home and all that stuff. Looked after me. I mean, he's six years older'n me, so it wasn't like there was anything between us that way. But he always treated me like his little doll. His little china doll. When I started drumming he would play with me, find something to hammer on, you know. We became a percussion duo—maybe the worst of all time, but that's what we were." She smiled reflectively. "Boonie was the one that found my first bass drum, the one his pa bought me for a dollar." Looking at me, she said, "You know why I smash the bass drum so hard? 'Cuz that first bass drum was so *small*. I mean, it must have been the littlest bass drum ever made! Like fourteen inches or somethin'. It wasn't until I left the Bransons and saw things on my own that I even realized that most bass drums are a lot bigger. Anyway, that little drum didn't make a lot of sound, so I had to stomp on the pedal really hard. Guess I still do."

"It's your claim to fame."

"Ha." She picked at a few bits of stray lint on her robe. "So, what happened was, Boonie's parents died in a car crack-up an' all of a sudden we were on our own." She shrugged. "We didn't know what to do. Boonie was old enough to work. He was eighteen."

"You were twelve?"

"Somethin' like that, yeah. But there wasn't any jobs around goddamn Bole, Indiana. So we decided to try the next town, and the next, and the next. This was...1940, I guess. In the middle of winter. We just left the house and started traveling together. Boonie could pick up work pretty easy."

"And you?"

"Me? I played on street corners. Just me an' my sticks. An' anything I could hit with 'em. The back of a bench. Cardboard boxes. The light pole. The edge of garbage cans. The sidewalk. Whatever. I got good, you know? I learned tricks—twirling the sticks in my hands, stuff like that. Tossin' 'em in the air like batons. People would laugh and clap for the little drummer girl. They'd give me things to play on—their handbags, the sides of their briefcases. An' they'd leave tips in the bowl I had there." She paused. "You get pretty independent, livin' like that."

"I'm sure."

"We weren't alone. Shit, you remember what it was like before the war."

"Sure I do."

"The war's what got everybody jobs. Great thing, I guess, if you look at it that way. Anyway, me an' Boonie traveled together for, I dunno, a year an' a half, somethin' like that. But Boonie started to become a little...I dunno. Different. Before, we were just like two peas in a pod, you know? My best friend. But...I guess some of it had to do with the fact that I was gettin' older. I wasn't that little girl anymore." She looked at me. "Know what I mean?"

"I think I do, Jeannie."

"Yeah. Well, it...changed things. Between us. I didn't mind. I mean, I *loved* Boonie. I would've done anything for him. I mean that. He was the whole world to me."

"I understand."

"But...you know, when his folks died in that car crash, he was in the car too. He was banged up pretty good. Spent a week in the hospital. And you know, when he came out he seemed just a little different, somehow. For a long time I figured it was just my imagination—I mean, we were both in shock from his folks dyin', he'd been hurt...and things were fine between us for a long time, but...I couldn't get this feeling out of my head that he was never exactly the same after the accident."

She stared at the sky again. "Maybe it had nothin' to do with the accident, but he got worse over time. Started gettin' mad a lot. Got into fights. My Boonie never did that kind of stuff before. But he changed. For a while he still protected me like he had. But then he changed with me too, I mean the way he was with me...Les, I owe Boonie my life. When my pa left, then his parents died, I had nothin'. *Nothin'.* Just a little hick girl with no family, no friends. Didn't go to school after the seventh grade. Think about how girls like that usually end up. When they have nobody. And they need money."

"I get it, Jeannie. He protected you."

"He *lived* for me. An' I lived for him. We were family. Each other's family. So when things...changed, that was okay. It made us even closer. But then..."

"He got violent with you?"

She smirked. "Damn near killed me, once. We were swimmin' in this dirty little lake somewhere in the Ozarks, where Boonie had a job. He held me under. It started as a joke. He was drunk. He'd push me under just for a second then I'd come back up and laugh. But he did it again and again, longer each time, till I was cryin' for 'im to stop, fightin' 'im, I couldn't breathe. Finally he just *threw* me up onto the shore and walked away. I didn't see him again for two days."

"What happened then?"

"Oh, he was a lamb. He was always sweet after he...got out of hand. Anyway, though, things were different after that."

"I'm sure."

"We were more distant with each other. I got a job in a fruit canning place, screwin' lids on jars all day long. Lived in a bunkhouse behind the factory with a bunch of other girls."

"Sounds awful."

"Are you kiddin'? It was *great*. I was on my own, Les. I'd just turned, I think, fourteen. But I had a job and a place to live. I was doin' better than a lot of guys that had families to support. Better than my dad, prob'ly."

"I see what you mean. Yes."

"So there was this little town near the factory an' at night me an' some of the girls would go there. There was a little place where bands played. We couldn't drink, but the owner would let us come in an' listen as long as we didn't go near the bar or try to get booze from the customers. There was this all-girl Dixieland band that played there, the Dixieland Honeys. They weren't very good, but, you know, they tried. A couple of 'em worked at the plant in the daytime. Well, their drummer went off to have a baby or somethin', an'—well..."

"Fate?"

She smiled. "I guess. Played the little house kit they had. That was the first real band I was in. I learned a lot there." She nodded. "It was great. We played three nights a week, just to local people, you know, never more than maybe twenty or thirty at a time. But we got better as we went along. I can still play some of those old tunes in my sleep."

"And Boone? He was in the army by this time?"

There was a long pause. Finally she looked at me.

"He was never in the army, Lester. He was in prison. He busted a guy up in a bar one night. Served three and a half years in Leavenworth."

"Oh my God, Jeannie."

"I'm sorry," she said, sighing, rubbing her temples. "I lied to you. I lied to Stan. I lied to everybody. I just...I wanted 'im to have a fresh start, you know? And I knew nobody would want an ex-con around. I thought he'd gotten better. I really did. So I thought...me an' Boonie both thought..."

She put her hands in her lap and sat unmoving for a long time.

"Jeannie," I said, "why did you want him around at all? After what he did?"

She was silent for a while. Then, in a small voice, she muttered: "'Cuz I love 'im."

○○○

After a few more days of recuperation Stan called Freddie and Hank and the Skye High Five continued, first with a few small gigs on Long Island, then in better clubs around New York City. We stayed off the road for a few weeks to give Jeannie more time, only playing places we could drive home from—that is, Stan's home—afterward.

One afternoon we pulled up to a big gray building on East 67th Street which turned out to be the WABD television studios. In 1945 the word "television" was still new to most people; I knew about it, had seen a few early sets here and there, but their tiny, washed-out gray pictures left me unimpressed and I was certain this radio-with-pictures device would prove to be no more than a novelty. (I was hardly alone in this.) And the war had all but killed this early technology, anyway: whatever stations had existed before, most were gone now, at least for the duration. But Dumont's WABD still broadcast several hours a day, and Stan had talked to a friend there and somehow gotten us on what was kind of a proto-talk show that featured various local personalities. I recall the studio as a mess of huge bulky cameras, thick cables, and flickering monitors everywhere. It was small and cramped, excruciatingly bright: when we took our positions I was all but blinded, and the heat from the television lights caused me to break out in a sweat before we even counted in the first number. Yet we had fun with "Flaming Spear," "Be With Me," and "All That Meat and No Potatoes." It was like a rehearsal; Jeannie and I had no real feeling of playing *to* anyone, and in fact, there could have been no more than a few hundred sets tuned into us that day. But without that nerve-wracking sense of playing for posterity that had hampered us when we'd made our record, we were loose and free. And nobody asked Jeannie to drum behind sound baffles.

It was a short gig but a terrific one, played, as far as we could tell, to only a handful of technicians and a couple of on-air people, all of whom applauded heartily. After the set the host talked to Stan and Jeannie for a moment—sticking the microphone in her face he asked her, "How do you feel about being called the female Gene Krupa?" to which she responded, "I dunno, how would *you* feel about being called the female Gene Krupa?" Then she added, "I love Gene Krupa. Gene Krupa's the best. But my name's Jeannette Crupiti."

We were invited back for the following week, and the week after; fun, yes, but it didn't seem very important, just a stopgap activity until we hit the road once more. Jeannie and I wandered around downtown New York a couple of times during this period and no one ever stopped us to say they'd seen us on television. I'm sure that very few had. WABD didn't record the shows—I don't know if they even had the technology then, but in any event there was no reason to—so we never saw what we looked like, translated grayly through the cathode ray tube.

At last we hit the road again, not seeing Stan's house for a month or two at a time. It was a heady period, with the band getting ever more attention. Jeannie returned to herself and, with no extra pseudo-cousin roadies around, we were like we'd been before, always together, heading out to clubs and movies everywhere we went, best friends again. In truth, that final tour is a blur in my mind. The clubs were even better than before and we seemed on the verge of a real breakthrough, never more so than one night early on in Indianapolis when, shortly before we were to go on, Stan found me and Jeannie at a table in the back. He had a little slip of paper in his hand that he gave over to Jeannie.

"Oh my God, have I been *drafted?*" she laughed, snapping her gum at him.

"Just read," he said.

She held it close to her face—I almost told her to put on her glasses, but didn't—and said, "Dear Stanley, good to see you're doing okay STOP, Saw my sister ha ha on television

STOP She is great STOP Can you open for GK Orchestra first week August Radio City STOP Tell your girl drum battle too STOP Best Regards Gene Krupa."

She didn't move. She just stared at the paper for a very long time. Finally I reached over and took it out of her hand, read it for myself.

"Gene Krupa?" I said at last, lamely. "*Gene Krupa* wants us to open for him?"

Stan nodded. "That's what the man says. And that's what we're gonna do." He smiled down at Jeannie, chucked her under her chin. "You got nothin' to say, kid?"

She looked up helplessly at him, her mouth partly open. She literally couldn't speak. Finally Stan laughed and said, "Take care of her, Lester," and moved off.

"Jeannie?" I touched her arm. "You okay?"

"Gene?" she said in a small voice. "Gene Krupa? I'm gonna play with Gene Krupa?"

"That's what it says," I told her, looking at the telegram again. " 'Drum battle too.' He says you're great. Because you *are* great. Radio City Music Hall! Gene Krupa! The Skye High Five!" I kissed her on her temple. "This is it, Bombshell. This is the big time!"

"Oh my God. Oh—my—God. Lester—" She looked at me, her eyes pleading, brimming with tears. "Lester, I can't do it. I'm not good enough."

"You *are* good enough, and you'll do it. It's time for the rest of the world to discover what I've known for a long time, Jeannie. What the whole band has known. That you're the best. The best there is."

"But...but *Gene Krupa*...? Lester, I...I'm just a hillbilly. I play barefoot and my cymbal used to be a hubcap on a fence post. I can't play with *Gene Krupa*. It's ridiculous. I'm gonna tell Stan to say no." She started to stand; I grabbed her wrist and pulled her down again.

"Lester, stop. I can't do it. I'm serious!"

"Jeannie," I laughed, "I'm only going to tell you this once."

"What?"

"Shut up."

◻◻◻

With the Radio City gig still months away, we kept on touring, stopping back home on Long Island only occasionally. Jeannie began working on new routines and tricks.

She had one I liked a lot. It had occurred to her that she was wasting the black stiletto heels she wore each night as she stepped onto the stage: "I just take 'em off and put 'em to the side," she said. "Then it hit me: Why not *use* 'em?"

And so she did. Keeping the rhythm up on the bass drum, she would lean down, pick up the discarded stilettos, and lift them high for the audience to see. Then, holding them by the toes, so that the spiky heels pointed downward—like hammerheads—she proceeded to play drums with them. Well, not *drums*: Jeannie learned early that stiletto heels would quickly puncture a drum head. Instead she played the cymbals. She had three, along with the high-hat, and she could bash out amazingly intricate rhythms with them, the heels themselves producing an unusual heavy tone when they struck the bronze of the cymbal.

This was notable enough, but she had another, even more surprising notion. With Freddie's help she rebuilt her high-hat in such a way that—unlike any other high-hat, in which the two cymbals can do nothing but move together and apart—on hers they could move in tandem all the way up and down the stand. This created a fantastic effect as Jeannie could step out from behind the kit and, whipping away on the thing with her sticks, she would appear to be bashing the cymbals right down almost to the floor. (In truth, she controlled the height of the cymbals with a separate foot pedal.) Then, like a swami summoning a snake from a wicker basket, she would coax them slowly back up. When they were where they belonged again she would flash a huge grin to the audience, which of course burst into cheers, and she would drop down behind the kit again and send us into the finish of the song.

This trick, spectacular in itself, did lead to some unexpected problems. It may be difficult to comprehend this now, but in 1945 women were not seen coaxing objects to rise up on a vertical pole unless they were on the stage of a burlesque house. It simply wasn't done. The first time I watched Jeannie perform her great high-hat routine, I thought it was the dirtiest thing I'd ever seen. Part of it was the routine itself, part of it the fact that her calves and feet were bare but for her sheer stockings as she did it; yet another was her round-eyed, round-lipped expression as the cymbals came up, an expression Marilyn Monroe would perfect a decade later in her movies. Jeannie wasn't *trying* to be provocative, not that way—she was just trying to put on a fantastic show. But it came out a bit differently. And it drove the men in the audience crazy, shouting, howling, yelling for her to "Do it, baby, do it!" I wasn't a fan of the routine, but I couldn't deny the lines that were starting to form wherever we played now, or the fact that the biggest uproar of the night came near the end, when Jeannie started in with her high-hat.

"Yeah, it's kinda silly," she admitted to me. "But Lester, you gotta admit it *works*."

◯◯◯

Then I saw Boone Branson again.

Or I thought I did.

It started in a sweaty, overcrowded club in Biloxi, everyone packed in to see the now red-hot Skye High Five. People were crowded in every available space, every table, all along the bar, standing room only—and dozens were standing. I could see people packed outside at the window, staring in through the glass. And for a moment I espied Boone Branson among them, just standing, not moving, in his old brown sports jacket and slacks, arms at his sides, dull fish-eyes aimed directly at the stage. I looked down at my guitar to negotiate a tricky chord change and when I looked back up again, he was gone. If he'd been there at all.

◯◯◯

It happened again in Houston, at a big, brightly-lit club festooned with colored lights and streamers and signs everywhere—not ours, ones they'd made themselves— proclaiming *Skye High Five—Best Combo in Jazz!* and *Houston Loves the Skye High Five!* and even *Welcome "JEAN KRUPA" World's Greatest Girl Drummer!* He was there—was he?—at the back, near the door. I couldn't be sure. The place was too crowded, too smoky, I was too busy keeping up with my parts. Yet I surely saw *some* large man, blockily built, in a tattered brown suit, one who just stood there staring, not shouting, not applauding, not dancing. Just standing. Just staring.

◻◻◻

I wanted to believe that it was my imagination, telling myself that there were countless thousands of large-built men who wore old brown suits. I hadn't gotten a clear look at the man in Biloxi or the one in Houston. They might have been anybody. I was hesitant to mention it to anyone, most of all Jeannie: we were having such fun again, the whole band one smoothly-oiled unit, everyone happy. Jeannie would spend hours at chess with Hank on his little magnetized board, beating again and again the guy who'd taught her how to play. When she wasn't doing that she was winning five or ten dollars a time from Freddie at gin rummy, and when she wasn't doing that she was in the back of the bus with me, just talking, napping, horsing around, reading my pulp magazines (she liked the horror ones best, especially *Weird Tales*). She drank endless Cokes, devoured endless potato chips and doughnuts—no results were ever visible on her slim, muscular physique—and, most of all, continually tapped out rhythms with her sticks on the backs of seats, on the cushions, on instrument cases, on my own head.

"I've decided you're right, Lester," she said once, reclining in her seat and tapping her sticks on the back cover of my latest issue of *Planet Stories,* which sat in her lap. "I can do it. I can play at Radio City with Gene Krupa. Who's that ol' Gene Krupa, anyway? I play better'n him. Well," she quickly corrected herself, "maybe not *better.* But I'm pretty good, ain't I?"

With anyone else this would have seemed naked compliment-fishing, but I knew with Jeannie it was her very real insecurity talking.

"You're better than pretty good," I said, tousling her hair. "Come on. You know that."

"Yeah, I guess." She grinned, playing a hard, tight roll on my magazine which succeeded in knocking a dozen little holes in the back cover. "I guess I'm pretty good."

It was moments like these that I desperately did not want to shatter by mentioning my suspicions to her about Boone Branson. But if I'd seen him, I reasoned, surely Jeannie would have too, and...And I remembered Jeannie's poor eyesight, along with her eternal refusal to wear glasses.

Then came the night in New Orleans when, after a gig, we all went out to the band bus and Freddie noticed something on the side, near the back. I saw him walk over to it, peer at it closely. I followed him.

"It's a bullet hole," he said, moving his fingers around its edges.

"Somebody shot at the bus?" I asked stupidly.

"Looks that way."

Everyone gathered around, Jeannie included. I impulsively put my arm around her.

She laughed. "Prob'ly just somebody jealous of us," she said.

Freddie jumped inside the bus, rooted around for a minute until he discovered what he was looking for: "It lodged in the seat here," he called through the window. He was standing at the back, the last seats before our gear took over the remaining space.

"Should we call the police?" I asked.

"Nah, let's just pull out," Stan said. "What the hell. It's New Orleans. Crazy people everywhere. Guns everywhere. Probably just some drunk fool taking potshots from the road."

"You're probably right," I concurred.

We left about an hour later, with no further incident. But I couldn't help noticing where the shot had hit—right near the back, where only two members of the band habitually sat. I was one of them. Jeannie was the other.

Boone Branson knew that.

○|○|○

And then the night in Santa Barbara when I woke at three in the morning and heard voices in the next room. Hers first. Then a loud, soulless monotone.

○|○|○

But by the time Jeannie stepped into the café where we'd decided to have breakfast the next morning, there was no trace of Boone Branson.

"Jeannie?" I said, after we'd ordered our eggs. "What's going on?"

"Hm? What do you mean?" She played with the ends of her hair, not looking at me.

"You know."

"I *don't* know, Spud."

"Boone. Boonie."

She looked at me then. "What about 'im?"

"I heard him," I said, keeping my voice low. "Last night."

"No, you didn't."

"In your room."

She scowled. She dropped the strands of hair and went to work picking at her fingernails instead.

"Walls are thin in that dump, huh?"

"Very thin."

She worked at her nails some more, furiously scraping and rubbing. "D'you think Stan would hire 'im again?"

"Jeannie!"

"He's better now. He feels real sorry for what happened before. That's why he wanted to see me. To tell me that."

"Jeannie, that's—it's—"

"You don't understand 'im," she said. "None of you do."

"I understand what I saw that night. I understand what you told me about the time he nearly killed you."

"That was a long time ago. The thing at the lake."

"Your split lip wasn't a long time ago."

"It wasn't all his fault. I said somethin' to him I shouldn't of."

"Jeannie, do you hear yourself talking? Are you listening to what you're saying? He *punched* you."

"Well, I've hit him a few times too."

"You're not his size."

"I'm strong, though." She smiled a little and flexed her bicep for me to see.

"This is serious, Jeannie."

She shook her head. "You don't understand."

"I understand fine."

"He just needs a little help. It's been hard for him since he got out of—" she lowered her voice—"out of prison. It's tough for somebody like that. And he's had bad breaks. But he ain't a bad person. Not really."

"What's your definition of a bad person, Jeannie?"

She frowned. "Hitler."

"Well, Hitler's pretty much done, from what I read," I said, gesturing at the newspaper next to me on the table. "Jeannie, you have to get Boone away from you. You should talk to the police. If you don't, I will."

Her eyes narrowed. "Don't. Don't you dare."

"I will. If you don't."

"I'm serious, Lester."

"So am I."

"I know how to handle Boonie. He's not workin' for the band now, so it's none of your business. Leave it alone."

"No."

"He hasn't done anything. Not anything."

"I don't trust him."

"I don't care. It's my life."

"Jeannie..."

"Promise me you won't talk to the police about Boonie. Any police. Anywhere we go."

I looked at her. "I'm not going to promise that."

"You have to."

"No, I don't."

"If you don't promise, Lester, we can't be friends."

"Jeannie, for God's sake..."

"Promise."

I sat back in my chair, feeling suddenly deflated. I dropped my eyes to my lap.

"No," I said.

I could feel her glaring at me. I kept my eyes down.

Finally I heard her chair scrape against the floor and she stood. I looked up again; she turned away and walked toward the café's front door.

"What about your breakfast?" I called after her.

Without looking back she said, "I ain't hungry."

○│○│○

I took a walk down to the ocean—we were playing a club on the beach, our hotel was attached to it—and I breathed the heady salt air for a while, trying to clear my head. Understand, no one used words like *stalker* or *dysfunctional* or *codependent* back then. I'd never heard of such things. All I knew was that I found Jeannie's behavior regarding Boone Branson completely baffling. And that Branson himself scared the living hell out of me.

We played two more nights in Santa Barbara, good gigs to healthy-sized crowds, and Jeannie did great. But she wasn't talking to me. In the hotel corridor, at the restaurant, in the bar: silence. Even as we tuned up to play she would say no more to me than absolutely necessary. Passing by me on the way to the stage there were no winks, no quick kisses on the forehead. There was no eye contact at all.

Well, I told Stan finally. Told him everything—about Branson, about her.

"Yeah," he said, swallowing his drink, "I thought I saw that guy one night. I don't know what we can do, kid. He hasn't done anything to get himself arrested." He scowled. "I wish he'd throw a punch at me. In front of a cop. I'd be willing to take one just to see him hauled away."

"Me too," I smiled grimly.

Up the road in Paso Robles we played a two-night engagement at a little hotel, a pleasant place, and none of us—eventually Stan and I clued Freddie and Hank in on what was happening—saw hide nor hair of Boone Branson. Jeannie was moody, sulky; it didn't affect her stage performance, but she requested a room at the other end of the hall from where the rest of us were staying and hardly came out of her room except to play. We left her alone; there didn't seem to be anything else to do.

And yet I do hold one moment from that brief engagement close to my heart. When we finished our last set, we took a group bow with Jeannie standing just to my left. Getting ready to step backstage, I turned left at the same moment Jeannie turned right; we nearly bumped into each other, which led to a quick moment of eye contact. It couldn't have lasted more than a second, yet something in her face softened in that second. She didn't say anything, she didn't smile, but she reached out her hand and touched my cheek gently with her palm before quickly stepping away and vanishing back to her room.

We loaded up the bus at the end of that second evening; we had to drive overnight to San Francisco to be available for a group interview and photo session Stan had arranged with some people from the *San Francisco Chronicle* first thing the next morning. We'd be playing the Fillmore, a huge place, just coming on then as one of the premier jazz destinations in the city; prominent critics like Rudi Blesh and Ralph Gleason were said to be coming to check us out and write reviews for the biggest West Coast publications. From there we'd be working our way back across the country over a span of a few weeks, playing a dozen engagements in the northern states and finally finishing in New York, with Krupa's orchestra at Radio City—and then taking a well-deserved break.

The Fillmore wasn't in the nicest section of town, but we were all sufficiently exhausted by the time we arrived that no one particularly noticed. We checked into the hotel across the street that Stan had arranged for us, Jeannie again taking a room far up the hall from the rest of the band. I fell asleep the moment my body reached my bed.

◖◖◖

The next morning I showered and dressed and wandered around busy Geary Street for a while, finally stopping in at a café for breakfast. I was still depressed about Jeannie, but maybe her little gesture meant something; perhaps we'd be friends again. In the meantime I was excited about the gig, certainly the biggest venue we'd ever played, and the attention from major reviewers—then the slow trip back to what would surely be our greatest triumph in New York.

When I got back when it was close to time for the photo shoot. I grabbed my band uniform out of the hotel room and made my way across the street to the Fillmore, where Stan had said the pictures would be taken. But before I got there I saw Stan, Freddie and Hank all standing by the bus in the parking lot and headed over to them.

"What's up?" I said.

But before anybody said anything it was obvious what was up. The door of the bus had been smashed in, glass lying everywhere around, the door itself shoved uselessly to the side.

"Damn," I said. "What did they take?"

"The drums," Stan said.

"The drums? Just the drums?"

"Just the drums."

"They didn't touch your sax, your trumpet...?"

"Just the drums. All the drums. The cymbals. Her whole kit."

I stepped into the bus, which seemed totally undisturbed except for the big drum cases being absent from their usual spots at the back.

"Wait'll Jeannie sees this," I said, returning to the guys. "Or has she been here already?"

"Ain't seen her yet this morning," Freddie said.

I thought for a moment. "I wonder if the Fillmore has a house kit she can use."

"Why *drums?*" Hank said. "Who steals drums? They could've had all Stan's instruments. Would've been a lot easier to carry. And to hock. Any pawn shop would take a good sax or trumpet."

"Shame," Stan said, kicking at the glass on the pavement. "Would've looked good for the photos. Her and her kit."

He told us he would find a phone in the building, call the police. Freddie and Hank agreed to watch the bus until they arrived. "Lester," our leader said, "go see if you can roust Jeannie out of bed, will you? Knock on her door."

"Sure." I moved quickly across the street, took the stairs, knocked on the door at the end of the hall I knew to be hers.

"Jeannie? C'mon, Jeannie, it's time to get up. Something's happened."

No response. I knocked again, hard this time.

"Jeannie?"

I stood there for a time, then marched thoughtfully back down the stairs and out into the street.

"She's not there," I called to the guys by the bus.

Feeling directionless, I stepped through the front door into the hall itself. Stan was there and passed by me with the owner of the place, on their way to inspect the damage and wait for the police.

I was alone in the building. It was dark, silent.

But then I heard a sound. Curious, at loose ends, I moved through the lobby area and passed through a set of doors, finding myself in the concert hall itself: a vast, cavernous place with hundreds of empty seats lined up facing the big stage. One spotlight was shining down on it; the rest of the hall was completely dark.

Jeannie's drums were set up on the stage.

I moved up the long aisle, relief and puzzlement coursing through me in roughly equal amounts. Her drums were safe; perhaps she'd awakened early, decided to get them set up, then gone wandering into the San Francisco streets...

But Jeannie would not have broken the bus door and shattered the window.

Reaching the edge of the stage, I stood there dumbly staring at the familiar pearl-colored kit with its "JC" crest on the bass head for what felt like a long time.

I heard a creaking sound behind me, the sound of somebody moving in one of the chairs. As I turned to look I saw, on one of the seats in the front row, only a few feet from me, a dirty brown sports jacket that had been tossed carelessly onto it.

He was there, standing before an aisle seat about six rows back.

"Hello, Lester," he said.

"Hi, Branson," I answered cautiously. "What's this all about?"

"What?"

"You visiting Jeannie?"

"Visiting Jeannie?" The same dull monotone I remembered, that I sometimes heard in my dreams. He looked odd without his sport jacket, but I could see through his shirt heavy sweat stains on his chest and under his arms, as if he'd been working hard.

"Yeah. Did you set up these drums, Branson?"

"I set 'em up."

"Why?"

Just then Stan stepped in through the lobby doors.

"Branson!" Stan shouted.

The huge man turned. "Yeah?"

Stan moved forward. "What the hell are you doing here?"

He gestured toward the stage. "Settin' up."

"What do you mean, settin' up? You don't work for me anymore."

"You got a gig tonight. Gotta get set up."

It was then that Stan realized that the drums on stage were Jeannie's. He moved toward them, passing Branson quickly.

"What the hell?" he said, reaching me, staring up at the drums. "Lester, you know anything about this?"

I shook my head.

He turned to look at Branson again. "You broke into my bus, you son of a bitch."

"Didn't have no key."

Stan's face was perplexed. He looked at me again. "Where's Jeannie?"

"I don't know. She didn't answer her door at the hotel."

"When did you see her last?"

"Last night, I guess. When we checked in."

He turned to Branson. "Where is Jeannie?"

And then, for the first and last time, I heard Boone Branson laugh. It was a strange sound, something like a bullfrog's chortle repeated again and again. It hardly sounded human at all. He did not smile when he laughed. His expression didn't change at all. His soulless eyes were the same.

Stan moved to Branson. "Where is she, goddamn it?"

"Right there," he said. "Ready for the gig."

"Where?" Stan looked around in the darkness and called, *"Jeannie?"*

"Ain't gonna answer you."

"Why not? Where is she, you crazy...?"

"Onstage."

Stan and I both looked. All that shone under the single spotlight were the pearly drums and golden cymbals.

"What? What are you talking about?" Stan demanded.

"She's onstage," Branson said again.

Stan moved quickly to the edge of the stage again, peered around.

"There's nothin' here but drums, Branson!"

"She's right there," he said tonelessly. "Get your instruments. Play with her. She wants you to."

"You crazy—what are you—"

And then Stan fell silent. He edged close to the drums, to the big bass drum. I don't know exactly what he saw there but his eyes widened and a low moan came from his throat. "No," he managed to say. *"No..."*

And Branson laughed his macabre bullfrog laugh and when Stan looked toward me with his face gray and suffused with horror I suddenly got it, got all of it, and in that moment I remembered what Boone Branson habitually kept in the pocket of his sport jacket and he saw me remembering and stopped laughing and stormed toward me but I was too close, I pulled the pistol from the pocket, raised it and, nearsighted, 4-F, never having fired a gun in my life, I pulled the trigger.

The police told me later that Boone Branson was dead before he hit the floor.

◖◯◗

I don't have many clear memories of what happened then. The police arrived almost immediately, having already been on their way because of Stan's call regarding the bus door; I recall just sitting there, in the seat where Branson's jacket had been, not moving. At some point I was in a small room in the police station being questioned; the other guys were in the hallway, all of them being taken off and talked to about what happened. I wrote out a statement, I think—or did one of the cops write it down for me?—and signed it. (This was well before the Miranda era; I had no attorney and didn't know to ask for one.) I seem to recall a beefy guy in a brown suit who reminded me slightly of Branson himself telling me that they weren't going to arrest me now, but, he said, "don't leave town."

I didn't leave town. Stan continued to pay for my hotel room until I was finally told no charges would be filed.

"Clear case of self-defense," the beefy guy said in his final interview with me at the station. "You're free to go, kid. Off the record," he said as he shook my hand, "the world's better off without a bastard like that. As far as I'm concerned, you did good."

◖◯◗

If Jeannie and I hadn't been on the outs, her room might have been next to mine, or at least next to Stan's. One of us might have heard something. There must have been *some* sound.

Surely a final argument, the sound of blows. But then again perhaps not.

No one would ever know when Branson slipped into what must have been a full-blown psychotic fugue (not that I knew such words in those days). For that matter, no one would ever know when he came into her room, or where from. Had they planned on being together? They certainly could have exchanged phone calls or even letters without any of the rest of us knowing. And Jeannie was hardly on speaking terms with any of us by the end.

In any event, when whatever went so terribly wrong went wrong, he killed her. Then he put the body in the bathtub and cut it into pieces, mutilating her so completely that a specific cause of death would never be determined. He might have simply stabbed her, or perhaps he strangled her first. No one ever knew.

Where did he get the tools to do what he did in the bathtub? Some he carried with him in his ever-present duffel bag. One, a big cleaver, he apparently stole from the hotel kitchen, along with some big burlap potato sacks. No one ever knew how he did this either. No doubt it wasn't that difficult, in the overnight hours when everything was closed.

If we'd been in a quieter, less urban environment he couldn't have done it the way he did. Just as he couldn't have gone out to the bus, broken open the door, and hauled all Jeannie's drums—it must have taken him at least four trips—to her room. The bus was parked in a dark corner of the lot but he may well have been seen; who was going to stop a man that size, or call the police, in a neighborhood like that?

He opened the various drums—he was quite familiar with the equipment—and put his terrible deposits into them, wrapped first in Jeannie's own clothing and then in the burlap sacks. Not everything fit, and what the police found in the room afterward was said to have made even the most grizzled veterans of the force physically ill.

Then he closed the drums up again, cleaned them off as best he could. He changed his clothes—a detail which shows some rationality still in his mind—and began carrying the instruments across the street to the Fillmore stage. By then it was early morning and the building was open. It would have looked perfectly normal to anyone passing by; surely people carried drum cases in and out of the Fillmore all the time. The manager didn't bat an eye when Branson told him he'd come to set up for that night's show.

Apparently I came across him not long after he'd finished, while he was resting from what must have been a hell of a strenuous night—strenuous enough for him to have taken off his ever-present brown sports jacket and leave it on that front-row seat.

◐◑◒

You might think that such a sensational case would have made headlines—at least in San Francisco, maybe nationally. You might think that Jeannette Crupiti would have ended up with a grisly kind of posthumous fame, the same kind of underbelly-of-the-business notoriety for which Elizabeth Short, the so-called "Black Dahlia," is still written about and remembered. But you'd be wrong.

Because on the same day that the events at the Fillmore occurred, President Franklin Delano Roosevelt died.

Jeannette Crupiti's killing, and Boone Branson's, hardly even made the *Chronicle*'s back pages.

◖◦◗

On the day the police officially absolved me of any legal culpability in Branson's death, the announcement came that Germany had surrendered. The San Francisco streets were packed with joyous, drunken revelers and the world was suddenly a new place, a place Jeannie would never see. I drank alone in my room that night, drank and cried. I quit the band the next morning and hitchhiked out of San Francisco. I've never been back.

◖◦◗

Three months later I was lying on my bed in my old room in Lonestone, Nebraska, listening to the news on my little radio when an announcer cut into the music and said that the war in the Pacific was over. Some new kind of bomb had been dropped on a couple of Japanese cities and that was it—total surrender. I said nothing, did nothing, felt nothing. I felt nothing at all for a very long time.

◖◦◗

And yet in the end Lonestone, Nebraska held no more future for me than it had a couple of years before, when I'd first left it behind. And a morning came when, this time supported by my parents to the point that they drove me to the station in Whitegate and hugged me and wished me well, I stepped onto a bus heading east, connecting eventually to another that would take me all the way to New York. I carried nothing with me but a few clothes in a rucksack; Stan had agreed to hold onto my things, including my trusty Gretsch Resonator and a couple of backups, until I came to Long Island for them.

"Whenever that is, kid," he'd said. "No hurry. I'll take care of your gear, don't you worry."

○○○

A brief search had been made for any of Jeannette's relatives, particularly the father she sometimes spoke of; but no one was ever found. In the end, Stan paid for Jeannie's burial in a little tree-shaded cemetery some fifteen miles from his home.

"The stone's not ready yet," Stan told me as we sat in his living room with drinks. I was amazed to think it had been less than four months since San Francisco; it felt like a century. The band was finished. Freddie was getting together his own combo, Stan said, and Hank had retired. Stan himself looked older. In place of the sparkle I'd once known in his eyes there was nothing but age and defeat. He'd loved Jeannie, just as I had—loved her for her personality, her innocence, her charm, her blazing talent. And he was aware, though he didn't say it then, that his last chance at a real comeback was done.

"I've been waiting," he said, "you know, in case a relative pops up, somebody who might want to put some words on the thing." He shrugged. "Nobody has."

"I think you could go ahead and do it, Stan. If anybody shows up later I'm sure they'd be grateful for your taking such good care of her."

"Yeah." He fished in his pocket. "Wanted to show you something, kid. The other guys said it was good, but when I got your letter that you was comin' I wanted to run it by you before I made the order." He leaned over and handed me a sheet of paper.

"What's this?" I said, unfolding it.

"Just look. It's what I got in mind for the stone." He watched me as I read it. "See, I couldn't decide—'World's Greatest Girl Drummer' or just, you know, 'World's Greatest Drummer'? I dunno. I hate the 'girl' thing. I mean, how many girl drummers are there? But I didn't want to insult Gene Krupa. Hell, he sent flowers to the funeral."

"I didn't know that."

"Yeah."

The sheet read, in block-lettered pencil:

JEANNETTE CRUPITI

1927 – 1945

And below that, just two words:

World's Greatest.

"It's fine, Stan," I said, my voice shaking as I handed the paper back to him. "It's perfect."

◎◎◎

It would be convenient to end this account by saying that I left music forever, moved back to Lonestone or off somewhere entirely different, became an insurance salesman or a plumber or a Merchant Marine (assuming they would have my five-two self). But it isn't true. In fact, I continued playing guitar, and maybe I was as good as Jeannie claimed: despite the oceans of guitarists who returned from Europe and the Pacific, I seemed to hold my own. I played in different combos and for a while in Tommy Dorsey's Orchestra—alas, in a period in the late forties when the machine-gunning Buddy Rich was no longer with them. But mostly I was a free-lance sideman, playing rhythm for any kind of jazz anyone might like to do: Dixieland, swing, bebop. I became fluent in all the styles and made a pretty good living; if you really want to hear me play, go to a vintage music store that specializes in vinyl and look through the credits on some of the releases of the '50s and '60s on labels like Vee-Jay, Contemporary, Pacific Jazz. Lots of times you'll see my name there in the small print—I did loads of session work in that period. And on those records, unlike the single unreleased disc cut by the Skye High Five, you can actually hear my guitar. The drums sound like drums, too. Though they don't sound like Jeannie's.

It's difficult to comprehend how much the world changed after Jeannie, and how *fast*—by the beginning of the '50s the war seemed a distant memory, what with men all marching off not to the battlefield but to their corporate offices in gray flannel suits, the women making babies at an unprecedented rate, the economy booming, everyone buying tract houses in the suburbs and cars and second cars and televisions and hi-fis with LP record players and stereophonic sound and guys who never would have imagined going to college doing so on the G.I. Bill. Of course one still saw, every now and then, a young man without legs in a wheelchair, a young man with a hook for a hand. But increasingly the world seemed to pass those people by, forget them. They seemed a leftover from the earth when it was still in black-and-white. We were in a new, Technicolor world now.

Increasingly it was a reality which had little use for Stanley Skye's brand of jazz. Bebop took over, swing mostly faded, the big bands died out; what was already seeming old-fashioned in 1944 was hopelessly outdated ten years later. Then came rock 'n roll, and the kids vanished from the clubs; jazz became an older person's music.

I can hardly imagine what Jeannie Crupiti would have made of it all.

Sexual mores changed in this period too, though not as quickly and, for a long time, not as openly. But by the mid-'50s the Beats were writing poems celebrating free love, including love among people of the same sex, and that began an earthquake which hit full-force in the '60s.

I continued to see Stan occasionally for years. He never attempted another comeback, though he sometimes jammed with his musician friends, including me, at the house. I sensed a restlessness in the old road warrior, and now and then he would wistfully put forward the idea of touring again with a new band. ("Including you, Lester," he'd say, "naturally.") But his health was declining and he just didn't have it in him anymore. Eventually he even stopped wearing his toupee, exposing the gleaming bald pate of an elderly man. He passed away in his sleep in the summer of 1962, hardly noticed by the press; he was buried in Connecticut, his birthplace, next to his wife. The funeral was sparsely attended, just a few family members and a couple of old jazzmen. Though I'd not been in contact with them in fifteen years, I knew that Freddie and Hank had passed long before. So I was the only member of the Skye High Five to be there. The sole survivor.

And Gene Krupa, Jeannette's hero, left us in 1973.

So did I ever lose my virginity? Yes. I was twenty-eight, but yes. Eventually I met a man who worked in promotion for Vee-Jay and we lived together in a little cottage on Long Island, only ten miles from Stan's place, for the next forty-six years.

He's buried on the other end of the cemetery from Jeannie; I'd hoped to place him closer to her, but there were no spaces there in the "old part" of the graveyard. Still, when I go to see him—and I do, often—I always go to see her, too.

How much longer I can visit them I don't know. I'm very old now, I have heart trouble, my hands shake, my eyesight is nearly gone. Up until a few years ago I played acoustic guitar two nights a week at a Holiday Inn nearby—pop standards, Beatles songs; no one ever requested "Be With Me," certainly—but that's impossible now. There is a young lady, Maria, who comes in to help a few hours each day, but it's all I can do to sit here typing this all out on this computer.

Occasionally when I'm channel-surfing, as I understand people call such activity with one's TV, I come across the cable station that runs old rock music videos. Though I dislike much of the music, I occasionally watch for a while, primarily to look at the drummers. Every now and then I'll see someone who reminds me, despite the differences in musical styles, of Jeannie. This happens with old videos of The Who, for example—their drummer was named Keith Moon, and his flying sticks and lightning speed and grins and grimaces can make me think just for a moment of Jeannie, Jeannie who would have been as big as any of them, as big as Gene Krupa—bigger—if...

But that was a black-and-white world, and we live in color now.

I have, by the way, never touched a firearm since that ghastly morning in 1945. I disapprove of handguns generally and would never have one in my home. But I've never regretted what I did that day for one single second.

Well.

There is a crisp, bright February afternoon outside my window today. In a few moments I'll finish here, shut off the computer, get my hat and coat, and walk out into the cold sunshine for a few minutes with Maria, who will hold my arm and make sure I don't fall. She's a trained nurse and I feel safe with her. We'll walk up and down the street, possibly a full block or even more, passing by the other houses of the neighborhood. The frigid air, I know, will feel good. It always does. But I'll tire quickly, and have to return far sooner than I want to.

When I'm back inside and fed and Maria has made sure I've taken my various medicines and has left for the day I'll sit in my chair in the living room and consider, as I often do, pulling out the single record ever made by the Skye High Five, think about putting it on the old player—I still have a machine that can play 78s. And then I'll decide not to, as I always do. The last time I did it, several years ago, the experience sent me into a tailspin it took me days to recover from. The sound is so awful, such a desecration of what the band was, what Jeannie was—playing that old record doesn't bring the Skye High Five back to life, it only makes us more dead.

But there's nothing else—nothing but some brittle newspaper clippings in an old album. I don't look at those, either. Jeannie is so very young and so very beautiful in the ancient photos but she's also trapped hopelessly in the '40s—her hairstyle, her makeup, her outfit. In truth she looks

242 | Christopher Conlon

a little strange to me now, like all women from that era do to contemporary eyes, and that depresses me more than I can possibly express.

Of course I'm totally incapable of looking at any photos of her which include her pearl-toned Slingerland drum kit.

And yet time has proven that what Jeannie once said to me was correct. Relationships never really end. Certainly mine with Jeannie never has. Her life, so filled with passion and verve and love, seems now to have been snuffed out so quickly that she hardly existed at all. The older I become the younger she seems to have been—the more fragile, the more helpless, the more in need of some final protection I was unable to give her.

But these are things for another time. Now I have my walk, my exercise, my good cold breathing. Everyone is gone, all those who meant anything deep in my life, but I'm still here. I hope that this account may help someone to understand what it all meant—what it *was*.

There's more life to live and I must live it.

So: one, two, three...

Count it in.

ABOUT THE AUTHOR

Christopher Conlon is best known as the editor of the Bram Stoker Award-winning Richard Matheson tribute anthology *He Is Legend,* which was a selection of the Science Fiction Book Club and which has appeared in multiple foreign translations. He is the author of several novels, including the Stoker Award finalists *Midnight on Mourn Street* and *A Matrix of Angels,* as well as three volumes of short stories, four books of poetry, and a play. A former Peace Corps volunteer, Conlon holds an M.A. in American Literature from the University of Maryland. He lives in the Washington, D.C. area. Visit him online at http:// christopherconlon.com.

CPSIA information can be obtained at www.ICGtesting.com
Printed in the USA
LVOW06s1553130813

347698LV00002B/257/P

9 780615 758183